Love is
a time of enchantment:
in it all days are fair and all fields
green. Youth is blest by it,
old age made benign: the eyes of love see
roses blooming in December,
and sunshine through rain. Verily
is the time of true-love
a time of enchantment — and
Oh! how eager is woman
to be bewitched!

THE WIDER SEA OF LOVE

Michael and Sarah are brought together by a chance accident. Their meeting, and the stormy clandestine ones that follow, change both their lives. They discover that there is no escape from a society whose prejudices condemn the relationship they have established. When crisis follows crisis Sarah's fears are realised: she must choose between her conscience and her marriage.

Books by Frederick E. Smith
in the Ulverscroft Large Print Series:

LYDIA TRENDENNIS
THE DARK CLIFFS
OF MASKS AND MINDS
THE GROTTO OF TIBERIUS
A KILLING FOR THE HAWKS

FREDERICK E. SMITH

THE WIDER SEA OF LOVE

Complete and Unabridged

ULVERSCROFT
Leicester

First published in Great Britain in 1969 by
George G. Harrap & Co. Limited
London

First Large Print Edition
published January 1992

British Library CIP Data

Smith, Frederick E. (Frederick Escreet), *1922–*
The wider sea of love. — Large print ed. —
Ulverscroft large print series: romance
I. Title
823.914 [F]

ISBN 0–7089–2580–4

Published by
F. A. Thorpe (Publishing) Ltd.
Anstey, Leicestershire
Set by Words & Graphics Ltd.
Anstey, Leicestershire
Printed and bound in Great Britain by
T. J. Press (Padstow) Ltd., Padstow, Cornwall

And if perchance I sail on that wider
    sea.
Think not, my love, that I love not
    thee.

1

SARAH ASHLEY was never certain why she turned off the main Bere Regis-Bournemouth road that late November afternoon. The lane that ran through the Great Heath and the Forest to Wareham would lengthen, not shorten, her journey home, and later she could put the impulse down only to her enjoyment of driving her car in bad weather. Grey mist settling in rime on gorse and hedgerows, wind soughing across the fields, winter darkness closing in fast: these things always made the tiny world of Sarah Ashley's car seem oddly snug and attractive.

She glanced at her watch. Just on four-thirty — she would still be home well before John. She decided to fry the rest of the previous day's steak for dinner. With Harriet and Robert coming later in the evening, it would make a quick meal.

She settled back and let herself enjoy the sense of movement, the hiss of tyres on the wet road, the strong pull of the engine. A crow, invisible against the black bark of an elm, took alarm and flapped away into the gloom. She was in the middle of the heath now and far-off lights shone with a frosty twinkle. As the road dipped and took her to the foot of a shallow hill she caught a glimpse of a small cottage of Purbeck stone. She had an impression of age, of tangled bushes and gnarled trees, before it passed from her vision. Surprise touched her for a moment: she had never noticed the cottage on this road before.

She was another half-mile down the road and approaching the spiky skyline of Wareham forest when her engine began to miss. As the coughing grew worse she pulled into the roadside but before the wheels had stopped turning, the engine choked and died.

She tugged at the starter but there was no response. She had never had this happen to a car of hers before and found the independence of her cosy world had suddenly vanished. Now it was a part of the bleak heath and the icy, fading sky.

Outside there were sounds one did not

hear within the car: the rustling of dead ferns gripped by frost, the cry of an animal caught by a stoat. She opened the bonnet in the hope a projecting wire would proclaim its guilt but from what she remembered of the engine everything appeared in its rightful place.

She stared uncertainly down the lane. She was an attractive woman of twenty-eight, expensively groomed from her black-and-white tweed coat to the modern, swept-back styling of her dark hair. Her figure and features were good, with dark, intelligent eyes and a sensitive mouth. She was frowning faintly as she tried to decide on her best move.

There was plenty of traffic on the Wareham road but it was at least two miles away. Alternatively she could wait inside the car until someone drove down the lane. But the heat had already drained from the Renault and she had no guarantee a passing car would stop.

It was only then she remembered the small cottage. It was a short way back along the lane and even if she received no mechanical assistance from its occupier he would surely have a car or a telephone.

She started to walk, fastidiously avoiding the mud that the autumn rains had brought to the road edge. Far in the distance there was a shrill wail, whether a train whistle or an animal cry she could not determine. The silence returned and the red lights of her car grew fainter, to vanish behind a bend in the road.

She had almost reached the cottage before the first car passed her and she made no attempt to halt it. Now standing in the lane outside the cottage, she regretted her decision. Driving past in her car she had gained an impression of age. Now she saw that neglect or poverty had also contributed to its dilapidation.

A rusted metal gate, with one hinge snapped and the other askew, was permanently open with its base buried in a heap of mould. Behind it the front garden was a wilderness of grass and weeds. Two unpruned apple trees stood on either side of the path, their aged trunks ivy-strangled. A half-hearted attempt had been made to harden the path by throwing down ashes and a few shovelsful of gravel but a pool of water glazed with ice still lay across it. The mist hid details of the cottage but it lay huddled behind its ivy-covered walls like a beggar in a tattered coat. Two windows, one upstairs and one down, were visible from the road but there was no light in either. The total effect was one of almost unbearable loneliness.

The girl hesitated as she remembered there was a cluster of foresters' houses another half-mile back along the lane. But she had intended to seek help at the cottage and there was a streak in Sarah Ashley that disliked running away from a decision merely because it had turned out unpleasant to perform. Frowning slightly, she started up the path.

To avoid the pool of water she had to step off into the long grass and felt its wetness through her nylons. She reached a patch of gravel and the crunch sounded loud in the silence. Honest with herself, she knew she was now hoping the cottage was unoccupied but as she passed a large hydrangea she saw there was a lean-to built along the side wall. It was made of old timbers and contained a motor cycle covered by a tarpaulin.

The front-door paint had flaked with neglect and left bare wood exposed to the mist. Below the window, an overgrown cottoneaster was bearded with rime. She could find no bell-push, only an old-fashioned door knocker down which drops of water ran like tears. She hesitated a moment, then swung it down.

The loud rat-tat made her start and the hollow echoes seemed to hang in the silence. Certain now that the cottage was empty she was about to turn away when a glow of light appeared in the uncurtained window on her left.

She realized it came from a door being opened in the rear of the cottage and felt the sudden, hard rapping of her heart. A moment later the front door opened and a man appeared in the narrow passage.

Yellow light, diffusing from a room behind him, served to hide his face but she could see he was slimly built and wearing slacks and a pullover. He stood a couple of feet back in the passage-way and something about his stance, the way he half-held the door between them, the slight bend of one leg, made her think of a wary animal. His sharp voice had undertones but they were too subtle for quick analysis. "What is it? What do you want?"

"I'm sorry to bother you but my car has broken down. Have you a telephone I could use?"

His posture of wariness did not ease. "No, I haven't. Sorry."

She realized now that he was about her own age. "Then could you possibly take a quick look at my car? It's quite a new one, so it's probably nothing serious. It's only a few minutes down the road."

He muttered something, then stepped back as if to close the door. His behaviour brought out her stubbornness, her desire to shame him. "Surely you'll at least advise me what I can do. It's a bitterly cold night to be stranded, you know."

For a moment she thought he was still going to refuse. Then, with immense reluctance, he drew the door open again. "All right. You'd better come inside."

Paradoxically she now wished he had refused her aid as she stepped into the dimly-lit passage. Ahead on the left was the open door through which the light was issuing. As he motioned her towards it she saw he had a gaping hole in the elbow of his pullover.

She entered the room ahead of him, seeing with a mixture of relief and apprehension that it was unoccupied. The furniture consisted of a chest of drawers, a settee, two odd wicker chairs, and, beneath the far window, a desk. A naked electric bulb dangling from the ceiling provided the light. She caught sight of a bookcase as she turned towards the man but then her eyes were held by his appearance.

She had been right, he was no older than herself. It showed in the slimness of his body, his unruly brown hair, in his pale, mobile face. At another time she felt he would not be unattractive but resentment, or whatever the emotion was that was upsetting him, gave him a sullen appearance. As he moved into the room she caught sight of a thin white scar that ran down his right cheek from temple almost to chin. In itself it was not a serious disfigurement but in his present mood it appeared to draw his moroseness and to give his mouth a bitter twist.

Noticing her gaze he turned his face sharply away, a reaction that told her much. Unable to judge how long she had been staring at him she spoke hastily. "I really am sorry to bother you like this. What do you suggest we do? Shall we take a look at the car first or would you prefer to find a telephone and contact a garage?"

He kept his face averted. "I'll go and look at it," he muttered. "You said it was only a few minutes away, didn't you?"

"That's all. It shouldn't take you long. Would you like me to come with you?"

His glance told her she had said something wrong. "No, I wouldn't. You stay here."

"But what if you can't get it started?"

"Then we'll phone a garage." He nodded vaguely at the wall behind her. "There's a phone along the road the forestry people use."

She hesitated, thinking of the bitterness of the night. "If there's a phone close by, wouldn't you prefer to ring a garage right away? It might save you a good deal of trouble."

He turned sharply towards her. "Why? Don't you trust me?"

"Trust you? I don't understand."

"Don't you trust me with the car? Because if you don't, damn well go and find someone else. I didn't ask you to come here."

Independent by nature, she was about to drop the car keys back into her handbag when something checked her. At the time she put it down to self-interest.

"It's not a question of trust — that's ridiculous. If you're willing to go I'm very grateful. I was only thinking of saving you the walk."

Once more he showed his dislike. "What are you worried about the walk for? I've walked to Wareham from here — I've done it often."

Bewildered by his conduct she decided the best thing was to say as little as possible. She handed him the car keys. "Very well. If you should need any tools you'll find them in the boot. I think there's a full set — they've never been used."

With his eyes still challenging her she believed for a moment he was going to withdraw his offer. Then he muttered something, snatched the keys from her, and made for the door. It was only then, with the light full on him, that she realized he walked with a pronounced limp.

The slam of the front door made her wince. Clearly he believed she had noticed his lameness earlier. Even so, it was difficult to explain such bitterness.

Left alone she examined the room more closely. An old-fashioned radio stood on the top of the chest of drawers with two framed photographs flanking it. One was of a young soldier, so self-conscious she knew the photograph had been taken in a studio. The other was the snapshot of a girl standing before a lake. She was wearing a plain cotton frock, her figure was not good, and yet there was a wholesomeness about her smile that made the picture attractive.

A cloth lay over the desk, covering some bulky object. On the floor close by was an untidy pile of magazines. A drip-feed paraffin heater stood in front of the empty fireplace. It looked as if it might have been found on a junk heap with its protective grille missing and the bodywork devoid of paint. It brought to her mind how chilly the room was, and walking over to it she found the wick was turned so low it was burning yellow.

She turned to the bookcase. The two top shelves were full of paperbacks, mostly crime and western fiction, and it was the lower shelves that held her eyes. Among the books there she saw a *King's English* by Fowler, a dictionary of synonyms, a *Whitaker's Almanack*, a popular encyclopædia, an anthology of English poetry, and a Shakespeare. The bottom shelf was mostly taken up by tattered volumes of classics, among them Dickens, Balzac, James, Stevenson, and Galsworthy.

A collection too motley, she felt, to be taken seriously: probably the serious works had been left to him by a relative and he had put them into the bookcase to make up space. At the same time they made her reconsider her impression of him and realize that his clothes and hostile manner might have made him appear more uncultivated than he actually was.

A glance beneath the cloth on the desk supported this view. An aged typewriter stood there with a few typed sheets alongside it, the top one turned over as if the man had torn it from the platen on her arrival and laid it defensively over the others. Lifting the cloth higher she caught sight of a large manilla envelope addressed to one of the more popular British magazines.

Although it seemed likely a morbid shyness had made the man throw the cloth over his work before opening the door to her, Sarah Ashley was now curious and being a woman would probably have read the typescript had not a sound outside the room made her start. It came from the closed door at the rear of the room and reminded her she had no grounds for assuming the man was alone in the cottage.

She went to the door and paused. The scrabbling sound came again, muffled as if it were coming from outside the cottage instead of from the adjacent room. Then she heard whining and realized the sound came from a dog trying to enter the cottage.

Pushing back the door and switching on the light she found herself in a small kitchen among poverty such as the sitting room had only hinted. The floor was of flagstones, the bare walls pitted with age and neglect. There was no furniture, only a blackened gas stove, a tea chest on which a mesh door had been fitted, and a shelf along the farthermost wall. A bread board with half a loaf and a knife stood on the tea chest and a few tins of food lay in disordered array on the shelf. A gas meter and a discoloured sink completed the fittings. There was an earthy smell and she saw the outer wall was damp-stained from ceiling to floor.

The dog outside had heard her and was renewing his scratching. The door had no lock, only a heavy pivoted latch that dropped into a socket on the lintel. She paused with her hand on it. She had no fear of dogs but the chances were great that anyone living in so isolated a cottage would possess an animal as much for protection as for company.

A moment later she was smiling at her fears as she pulled the door open. The dog that fell inside was a small black Scottie. With tail whirling it was clearly about to make a tremendous fuss over its master and when it saw her, a stranger, it almost fell over backwards in dismay. It bolted across the kitchen, then, remembering its duty, turned and let out a timorous bark. When she held out her hand it hesitated, then came cautiously forward, eyes suspicion-bright beneath bushy eyebrows. It jumped back a foot as she attempted to stroke it, then sniffed warily at her ankles. This time it allowed her to caress its ears before drawing back.

Laughing, she went down on her heels. "That's better. Now we're friends, aren't we? What's your name?"

The dog whimpered uneasily and wandered on its short legs into the sitting room. Before closing the back door she glanced outside. Although the light had almost gone she caught sight of high, tangled grass, a few gnarled fruit trees, and through the mist the shadow of an encircling hedge. Hearing the distant screech of a vixen she gave a shiver and hastily latched the door.

When she returned to the sitting room the dog was scratching at the front door and she went out to it. "It's all right.

Your master hasn't left you — he'll be back in a few minutes."

It was strange, she thought, as she sank somewhat gingerly on to the torn settee, how a dog's affection for its master could influence one's own opinion, whereas in fact the very completeness of a dog's devotion made it useless as an index.

She found herself glancing through the magazines that lay on the floor. They were an odd mixture, with a high proportion of women's magazines among them, but believing she now understood the man's reason for having them she felt no surprise.

As the chill of the cottage sank into her she gave a sudden shiver and drew her coat more tightly around her. Remembering seeing a paraffin can in the kitchen she thought of filling up the oil stove but on going back for it she discovered there was no fuel. She was frowning when she returned. She had never equated poverty in modern Britain with a lack of heating fuel.

It was the glad barking of the Scottie at the front door that told her the man had returned. As the door opened and

16

the dog leapt and scampered around him he gave her a terse nod. "Your car's going again. I've brought it back with me."

"Oh, well done. I am grateful to you."

The mackintosh he was wearing was threadbare and stained. He shrugged it off, threw it down on the staircase, and rubbed the excited dog's ears. Then he turned to her.

"Here are your keys. You shouldn't have any more trouble."

She realized she had been right — it was his sullen manner more than his voice that made him seen uncouth. He had something of an accent — she was not expert in them but believed his derived from Yorkshire but his use of words appeared adequate enough.

To prevent his ushering her out without further ceremony she had deliberately left her handbag in the sitting room. "What was wrong with the car?"

She did not miss the quick glance he gave the desk and was glad she had been careful in replacing the cover. "Nothing much," he muttered. "Only a bit of grit in the carburettor."

"All the same, it was clever of you to find out so quickly. Are you an expert on cars?"

The scar, pulling at the nerves of his face, gave him an expression almost of contempt. "It doesn't take an expert to clean out a carburettor."

"You still have to know it is the carburettor. I didn't."

His silence, contempt by implication, gave her a twinge of irritation. Wondering how much of his surliness was natural and how much due to shyness, she pointed down at the fussing dog.

"I hope you didn't mind my letting him in. He was whining at the back door."

"No. That's all right."

"Where had he been? I didn't hear him bark when I arrived."

"He'd probably been for a run across the heath," he muttered. "I usually take him for a walk in the afternoons and let him loose afterwards."

She wondered how to get him talking about the typewriter on the desk. She nodded towards the bookcase. "You have a lot of good books. Do you read much?"

She felt the lightning glance of his eyes. "A little. Why?"

It was his suspicion that defeated her. Why? She could think of no answer to that. "I just wondered, that was all."

He moved back to the door. His limp was not ungainly; his slim body made it an almost graceful movement. His hand settled on the door knob, a blunt hint for her to leave. Conscious she was defeated, her hesitation came now from the feeling she ought to reward him. She fumbled in her handbag and pulled out a ten-shilling note. "I hope you'll do me another favour and accept this. I don't know what I'd have done if you hadn't helped me."

His sudden anger made her flinch. "What the hell do you think I am — a beggar?"

She made the mistake of arguing. "It's nothing. It would have cost me four times as much if I'd called in help from a garage."

The virulence of his contempt dismayed her. "People like you are all the same, aren't they? Money's your answer to everything."

"I don't know what you're talking

about. All I want to do is repay a debt."

"And money's your way of doing it! Keep your ten bob and anything else you've got in your damned purse. I don't want any of it."

She walked past him into the passage, her face white with anger. In her frustration she could not pull open the front door and had to wait while he limped past her. It was this fresh sight of his ragged clothes, his disability, and his sullen, ashamed face that, to her surprise, gave her a new tolerance.

"Look, I didn't mean to insult you. I only wanted to show how much I appreciated what you've done. Surely you must have been in similar situations yourself when you haven't been certain what to do. I'm sorry. Truly sorry. I can't say more than that, can I?"

His response, sullenly hesitant as it was, seemed a victory in itself. "All right," he muttered. "Forget it. Only I can't stand people who think money's the answer to everything."

"Nor can I. But this wasn't meant that way." The Scottie was still fussing round his feet and in an effort to relieve the tension she bent down to pat it.

"What do you call him?"

"Robbie."

"Robbie. It suits him. Goodbye, Robbie. Thank you for keeping me company while your master was away." She straightened, wanting to talk more but again defeated by his isolation. "Well, goodbye, and thank you again for your help."

The mist, tinted by the escaping light, was like yellow smoke as she stepped outside. At the gate she glanced back. He was still gazing after her but then, as if ashamed to be seen, closed the door sharply, and she was left in a grey limbo.

The car engine was warm and fired immediately. She glanced back a last time, suddenly realizing she did not know his name. The cottage, huddled behind the frozen hedges, was once more in darkness. Mist swirled in arabesques in the beam of her fog lamp as she drove away.

She switched on the heater and a moment later warm air was flowing deliciously around her ankles, a pleasure marred almost immediately by her memory of the inadequate paraffin heater. She was driving fast and wondered why — there was still three hours before Harriet and Robert were due.

2

IT was six o'clock when Sarah turned into Ferndale Avenue. Their house was the sixth down the Crescent, pebble-dashed, with twin bays and a double garage, a house the estate agents Marks & Marks had offered John Ashley when transferring him to the management of one of their Bournemouth offices two years ago. As she turned into the gravel drive the open garage doors told her John was home.

She pulled in alongside his Humber. The side door was unlatched and as she entered the house the centrally-heated air pushed back the winter night. Removing her coat she glanced into the sitting room. She thought John might be watching the news but the television screen was dark. Nor was he in his study alongside the cloakroom. She walked up the hall to the foot of the stairs. "John? Are you upstairs?"

His muffled voice reached down to her.

"Hello, darling. I'm in the bathroom — I won't be long."

Although he would only be washing his face and hands, she knew as she walked upstairs that the bathroom door would be closed. John had always been prim that way, compelling her to similar conduct, but now, after seven years of marriage, she was beginning to wonder if he was not right. Perhaps in the end nothing did destroy respect more than over-intimacy.

Opposite the closed door of the bathroom was their bedroom with its candlewick-covered double bed, its satinwood suite, and its heavy brocade curtains. Crossing over to her dressing table she stared at herself in the mirror. Did she look more than twenty-eight, she wondered? Perhaps when one was married to a man thirteen years older than oneself and moved in the circle of his friends one tended to dress that degree more conservatively. But why was she having these ideas now? Because a young man had shown as much interest in her as if she had been seventy and been eager for her to leave his cottage? She smiled at the thought.

John entered the bedroom a minute

later. He had put on a clean shirt and was buttoning up the sleeves. With the image of the young man still in her mind she thought how healthy and prosperous her husband looked. A little over-fed too — lately she had detected the first hints of a thickening waistline — but the thought seemed disloyal and she thrust it aside.

She knew exactly what he would do and he did not fail her. He kissed her forehead just in front of the right temple and patted the back of her right shoulder, a gesture as familiar as the way he combed his fair hair or knotted his tie.

His fresh complexioned face had a polished look and he smelt of toilet soap. "Hello, darling. You're later than usual. Did Eunice keep you talking again?"

Eunice was her friend in Bere Regis whom she visited once a week. "No," she said. "I had a breakdown on the way back."

He had been walking towards his tallboy. Now he halted and turned. "Not an accident!"

"No. The engine spluttered and died. It was only dirt in the carburettor. But it took me some time to get help."

"What did you do — phone the A. A.?"

"No, it was a lonely stretch of road and I couldn't find a kiosk. But a young man in a cottage fixed it for me."

"Where did this happen?"

She was about to tell him when the young man's expression on being offered payment came to her. John had something of a fetish about being in people's debt and if he knew the address it was not impossible he might call round at the cottage when he was in the district.

"Somewhere on the Wareham Road," she said, opening a drawer of her dressing table. "I can't say just where — it was quite foggy."

"I suppose you gave him something for his trouble?"

She felt a slight burn of irritation at being forced into a lie. "Yes. Ten shillings. Although he didn't want to take it."

He nodded and began humming as he took a handkerchief from his tallboy. "You sound happy tonight," she smiled. "What are you hiding from me? Good news?"

His laugh was self conscious as he turned towards her. "I suppose I am. Do you remember that big plot of land in Wallesden we've been stuck with all these years? Well, a couple of weeks ago I was tipped off that a big Oxford manufacturing company were looking for a plot down here. I drove up to see them last week and, to cut the story short, I'd a phone call today to say they've bit, hook, line, and sinker."

She tried to sound enthusiastic. "That'll be quite a feather in your cap, won't it?"

"It won't do me any harm at head office, seeing the previous manager had it on his hands for three years. And there'll be a fat commission, of course."

Harriet won't like that, she thought, allowing herself a moment of malice. She'll pretend to be delighted but there'll be something in her smile that'll make it look as if her suspender belt has broken. And the acid will come out when she talks to Robert. Poor old Robert — there was no commission for a bank cashier and Harriet had never forgiven him for it.

It was then she remembered the phone

call that morning. "Your mother rang to ask if we'd go round on Monday evening — apparently she has a friend who'd like your advice on buying property down here. She thinks it could mean a bit of business for you."

He nodded enthusiastically. "That's all right. We're not doing anything on Monday, are we?"

His mother, Lena Ashley, was a sprightly sixty-year-old widow. Sarah had sensed her rivalry soon after meeting John but in those days had been too idealistic to believe a possessive mother-in-law could pose a threat to a love marriage. Since she had discovered the truth it had been like a game of chess between them, with Sarah encouraging John — who seemed quite oblivious to what was happening — into making escapist moves and Lena Ashley grimly countering them.

They had moved to the other side of Nottingham — Lena Ashley had promptly taught herself to drive and bought a car. They had moved down to Bournemouth and not six months later Lena Ashley had bought a house just half a mile from them on the pretext her doctor had ordered a change of air. Now, with John going from strength to strength in his estate office, no further geographical escape seemed likely.

At least, Sarah thought, she was the kind of woman who prevented one getting too depressed that one had no children of one's own. Trying to dominate John as if he were still a child, touting business for him as if he were still a junior salesman — if motherhood did this to a woman it was possible to find some solace in one's deprivation.

"I don't think I'll go, if you don't mind," she told John. "You'll want to talk about property and I could use the evening to finish my dress. Your mother won't mind."

His face clouded. John was a great one for 'togetherness' and always saw a rebuff in any unwillingness of hers to share his leisure time. "Are you sure? We won't be talking about property all night."

"I would prefer to finish the dress, darling. I won't get a chance over the weekend."

He looked disappointed but was humming again by the time she went downstairs. Smiling to herself, she decided his sale that afternoon must have been a very good one indeed.

Harriet and Robert were later than usual that evening and Sarah could tell at once they had been quarrelling. There was that malicious bite to Harriet's voice each time she addressed him. Robert, prematurely balding, bulky of build, was sitting in the armchair opposite her, with Sarah and John sharing the settee. Harriet's anecdote was typical of her mood.

"Did you know the old spinster who lives opposite us is trying to seduce Robert?" Her violet eyes challenged her husband for a moment. "You don't mind if I tell them about it, do you, darling?"

Robert took his pipe from his mouth, hesitated, then as if realising the futility of protest, replaced it and grinned somewhat sheepishly at Sarah.

"She's just like the old maid you've got next door to you," Harriet said. "Tall and angular, with huge, huge feet. The sort that look as if they've been forty all their lives."

Charity, Sarah thought. Does she ever

feel any? Watching her, petite, blonde, fashionably dressed, her feet curled up beneath her in the armchair, Sarah wondered what mystical attraction could have brought her and Robert together. The fascination of the large for the small, perhaps? The amiable for the waspish?

She felt instant shame. Harriet wasn't as bad as all that. When she, Sarah, had gone down with 'flu last year Harriet had been the first to offer help. It was the sharpness of her teeth that was her trouble and the way she seemed to enjoy cutting them on Robert.

"I've seen her watching Robert before," Harriet was saying. "And on Monday evening she came across to say one of her fuses had blown and she didn't know how to fix it. Robert was over like a shot and there wasn't a glimpse of him for the next hour. What went on in the dark I can't imagine, but she's been giving him the coyest of looks ever since."

As John laughed, Robert gave another embarrassed grin. He secretly hates this kind of leg-pulling, Sarah thought, and was glad when John came forward with another round of drinks. She did not miss the how-charming-of-you-darling look Harriet gave him as she accepted her dry martini. She would be in bed with John like a shot if given the chance — Sarah had known this a long time. While the joke was on Harriet — she seemed not to have grasped John's inherent puritanism — it did not always make her company easy to bear.

It was a relief when they had gone and Sarah could drop into bed — a headache had bothered her for the latter part of the evening. John, always considerate at times like this, was quietly getting undressed and was beside her in bed in less than five minutes.

The double bed was an indirect legacy from a comfortably-off aunt of John's who had given them a bedroom suite as a wedding gift and at the time, Sarah felt certain, neither of them had liked to refuse the bed for fear of hurting the other's feelings. An opportunity for a change to single beds had come two years ago when they bought a new bedroom suite but in marriage some things become more difficult to suggest as the years pass by and another double bed had been the outcome. Sarah herself did not mind it too much: there were obvious disadvantages but she was womanly and sensual enough to enjoy the warmth of John's body alongside her, particularly during the winter nights.

It was John, with his ambivalence towards sex, who she felt might prefer single beds. He had always been an inhibited lover: even after seven years of marriage he had never seen her entirely naked. Sometimes when making love to her he would seem about to throw off the covering sheet but always it would somehow remain and hide them.

He suffered, as she had long realized, from a secret shame of sex that she, like many other women, had never experienced. Shyness, yes — he had made her that — but this she knew could have been conquered by the healthy attentions of an unembarrassed lover. In humorous moments she attributed John's inhibitions to his parents. Photographs showed his father to have been a small and physically inconspicuous man. With Lena Ashley powerful and masculine, perhaps some complex hormone antipathy had been aroused whenever she had been compelled to lie down beneath him in the love act, and this antipathy had passed down through her bloodstream to John.

Thoughts of this nature were not frequent in Sarah, nor were they damaging. Part of her — perhaps the part conditioned by the same society that had conditioned John — tended to respect him for not making a fetish out of sex. She accepted him as a normal husband and normal he was by accepted standards. Certainly — and here was the ambivalence — he could be quite demanding when his inhibitions were temporarily dulled.

Beside her, he had turned over and laid a hand on her shoulder. As it moved down as if to cup one of her breasts she wondered if he was going to make love to her. He had drunk at least five whiskies that evening and as he was normally a small drinker — alcohol tended to act on him as an aphrodisiac.

If it was his intention his sleepiness proved too much for him. His hand rose again and ruffled her hair affectionately.

"Night, night, darling. Sleep well."

"Good night," she whispered.

He was asleep within two minutes, a talent she had long envied. Lying there in the darkness she found herself thinking again about the lame young man she had encountered that afternoon.

His poverty and isolation, and his apparent hostility towards anyone intruding on that isolation, had awakened her curiosity. His contemptuous remark about money had also intrigued her and made her wonder what kind of a man he was. As sleep approached, bringing with it ideas more fanciful, the thought came to her that his hostility might have carried an undertone of despair. She dismissed the idea as melodramatic but at the same time knew that under one pretext or another she wanted to meet him again.

3

SHE paid a visit to the cottage the following Tuesday. Tuesday was Eunice's birthday and because her husband, a constructional engineer, was up in Lancashire working on a contract, Sarah had promised to spend the day with her. She took the longer road to Bere Regis and drew up outside the cottage just after 1:30 P.M.

It was a bitterly cold day and on the heath opposite the cottage the paths of forestry tractors were delineated in ridges of frozen mud. She shivered and drew her coat closer around her as she closed the car door. The wind was as cutting as a knife. As she walked gingerly down the muddy path she heard the muffled bark of a dog from inside the cottage.

The barking grew louder as footsteps approached the front door. She heard the lock turn and the door half–opened. He stood behind it in the defensive posture he had shown on their first encounter. At first he seemed not to recognize her.

"Hello," she said, smiling. "Remember me? I'm the person you helped last week."

He nodded curtly. "What are you doing here?"

"I've a friend in Bere Regis I visit once a week. That's why I was driving past here last Thursday." Her gaze was drawn to the Scottie who had pushed past his legs and was looking up at her with bright, curious eyes. "Hello, Robbie. Do you remember me?"

The dog sniffed at her outstretched hand and then began to wag its tail. She laughed.

"Look, he does remember. Wait a moment, Robbie — I think I've got something for you." Pulling a bar of chocolate from her handbag she broke off a piece and held it out. The dog's enthusiasm told her she had found its weakness. The man bent down and caught it by the collar.

"That's enough, Robbie. Come back inside." He faced the girl again. "You haven't said what you want."

The wind, rustling the dead leaves

of the hedge and making her shiver, provided the excuse she needed. "Couldn't I come inside for a moment? It's very cold out here."

He hesitated, then limped reluctantly to one side. As he followed her into the living room she turned to him. "You know, the only one of us who was introduced last week was Robbie. My name's Ashley, Sarah Ashley."

He appeared to flush slightly. "Mine's Michael Lindsay."

"Lindsay's a Scottish name, isn't it?"

"I don't know. I was born in Yorkshire."

"What part?"

"Doncaster."

She was doing well, she thought. "I always thought Yorkshiremen believed there was no place like Yorkshire. What has brought you all this way south?"

She was to learn to her cost that to ask him questions about himself was like probing for a passage through a minefield. One false move and the ground was likely to explode in one's face.

"What do you want to know that for?"

"I'm sorry. I didn't mean to be curious."

A nervous spasm was distorting the scar that ran down his cheek. "I'm here because I wanted to get as far away from the damned place as possible. Does that make you any happier?"

"Please. I have apologized. I couldn't know an innocent question like that would upset you, could I?"

He muttered something and turned away. "I'm not upset. I just don't like talking about it, that's all."

Standing there in embarrassment she wondered again what her motives were for paying the visit. As she saw the uncovered typewriter on the desk she remembered her excuse.

"Don't think me curious again but the other evening I couldn't help thinking you might be a writer." As he started she shook her head. "No, I didn't read anything — I guessed it from your typewriter and the pile of magazines near the desk. Am I right or wrong?"

The eyes that stared aggressively at her were brown with hazel specks in them. Eyes that, in spite of their hostility, seemed curiously defenceless.

"What's it to you what I am?"

"I had a cousin once who used to write short stories," she explained. "I was feeling rather depressed at the time and she thought writing might help me. She gave me books and advice but it was no use — I hadn't the talent for it. But I did learn some of the problems of writing and I also developed an interest in it."

She felt he was trying to decide whether to believe her. "Is this what you came round to tell me?"

"No. I wondered if you'd care to have the books. They're no use to me these days."

His hostility made her flush. "I'm a scribbler, yes. Like thousands more. But who the hell gave you the idea I need any help?"

"I'm sorry. I didn't mean it that way." Then her embarrassment turned into temper. What did he think she was — a frustrated woman looking for seduction?

"I offered you the books because you did me a favour last week and I'd like to show my appreciation. But if you don't want them you've only to say so. There's no need to bite my head off."

Looking back on it later, she realized it was her resentment that succeeded where her earnestness had failed. He frowned, then shrugged. "All right, if it'll make you feel better. It won't do any harm to read them, I suppose. Have you got them with you?"

She moved stiffly to the door. "No. I only thought about them last night and I've had no time to look for them yet. I thought I'd bring them when I visit my friend again on Thursday. I'll be passing here about 11:30. Will that be all right?"

He limped after her to the front door. "Yes, I'll be here. Thanks."

She was still angry with him when she climbed into her car but the sight of him, thin and pale, retreating into the empty cottage changed her mood and for the rest of the drive to Bere Regis she found herself puzzling yet again at the circumstances that could have brought a man of his age to live in such isolation. It was a welcome relief to spend the rest of the afternoon with Eunice, down-to-earth and uncomplicated.

She had met Eunice at a party two

years ago and, helped by a mutual love of music, they had become good friends. With Eunice possessing no car of her own, Sarah had fallen into the habit of driving into Bere Regis every Thursday and having lunch with her.

A year younger than Sarah, Eunice was plumpish and vivacious with a freckled face, light-brown hair, and a sunny disposition. Sarah liked her because in general she lacked the malice that marred so many other women of her acquaintance. Her marriage was only two years old, and the enforced absences of her husband, although bitterly bewailed by Eunice, had the effect of prolonging its honeymoon qualities. It was the difference in the time the two girls had been married that sometimes made Sarah feel an older woman.

She had brought Eunice a long-playing Klemperer record for her birthday and with her usual enthusiasm Eunice was delighted with it. She showed her disappointment however, when, just after 3:45, Sarah rose to leave.

"Isn't it rather early? Couldn't you have a cup of tea first?"

"I'd better not. John's got a dinner date for us tonight in Weymouth with a business friend of his, and he asked me to be back in good time. It's quite a long drive, particularly in this weather."

"I suppose you couldn't manage to get round one evening?" Like most extroverts Eunice was lost on her own. "Maurice isn't due back for weeks yet and time drags like hell."

Sarah looked doubtful. "John's got us booked up pretty solidly this week but I might manage something early next. I'll do my best and give you a ring."

On her arrival home Sarah found John in the sitting room reading the evening paper. "Hello, darling. You're back from the office early, aren't you?"

He lowered the newspaper. "I didn't like the look of the weather, so left early to give us more time." Then he noticed her expression. "What's the matter? Have you another headache?"

She nodded. "It came on as I was driving home."

"You've been getting a lot of them recently. Let me phone the doctor tomorrow to give you a check-up."

43

It was the moment she almost told him about Michael Lindsay. To seek his advice, to share the responsibility she now felt oddly burdened with. A moment that, no matter how it had turned out, would have saved them both the anxiety and the unhappiness that lay ahead. His concern made her smile.

"I don't think there's any need for that. But I wish we hadn't to go out tonight, particularly all that way. We couldn't put them off, could we?"

He looked startled. "At this time? They'll have everything ready for us."

"Then why don't you go on your own? Explain to them I'm not feeling well."

He shifted uncomfortably in his chair. "Take a couple of aspirins and lie down for half an hour. At least try it and see how you feel. I don't want to offend Prentice, or his wife for that matter. He's in a position to put a good deal of business my way."

The impulse to confide shivered and was gone. John, conservative, sleek with success, meeting and talking to the hypersensitive and hostile Michael. At that moment she felt it would be as disastrous as introducing a well-fed Labrador to a half-starved cat.

She walked over to a decanter and poured out two glasses of sherry. A restlessness she had felt for over a year seemed to have crystalized and she felt quarrelsome without being certain of the reason. As she walked back towards him she heard her voice.

"I hate Prentice. He's a fat little snob and so is his wife."

He looked startled by her outburst. "How can you say that? You've only met him a couple of times."

"I can tell a snob if I meet one for only two minutes. Prentice is a snob and all he thinks about is money."

About to protest further, he shrugged instead. "All right, what if he is? We're not going out for his company — we're going to do business with him."

She handed him a glass of sherry. "That's the thing I don't like. We do it too often. We ought to spend our evenings with people we like. This damned affluent society is dehumanizing us."

He stared up at her. "Dehumanizing us? What on earth are you talking about?"

"I'm saying we're putting too much value on money. All of us. The richer we grow the less we seem to want people as friends. If we go on like this we'll be like predatory animals, only going out when we're on the hunt."

Looking alarmed he rose and put his arms around her. "That's a bit of an exaggeration, isn't it? How often do I ask you to do a thing like this?"

At least twice a week, she thought, and immediately reproached herself. You're exaggerating. You're a stupid, emotional fool. But just the same, can't he see there's a grain of truth in it? His arms tightened around her.

"I've noticed you've been a bit edgy lately. I'll phone the doctor tomorrow. Even if there's nothing wrong you could do with a tonic."

She shook her head impatiently. "I don't need a doctor. It's nothing like that."

"Then what is it, darling? What was all that about?"

Wondering why she was gripping his arms, she drew back with some embarrassment. "I'm sorry. I suppose I was talking nonsense. Don't worry — we'll go tonight."

Showing relief at her recovery he pulled her closer again and kissed her. "I think we made a mistake in only taking a week's holiday this year. How about going to Italy next summer and getting some sun again?"

It seemed only a small part of her mind was listening to him. "Yes. That would be nice."

"Then that's what we'll do. We'll take three weeks and let our hair down."

If you judged a man on the limits of his understanding, she thought — and how else could you judge him? — then no-one could be more generous than John. She felt nothing but affection for him at that moment and yet was relieved to go upstairs to her bedroom where the air was cooler.

4

THE following morning she found one of the books she had promised Michael — a slim volume giving advice on writing for television. Unable to find the other she went out and bought a larger work on the art of short-story writing. An impulse made her also buy a ream of typing paper and a dozen carbons.

She had not been home more than a few minutes before she heard a car entering the drive. A glance through the sitting-room window showed her a bare-headed, sixty-year-old woman climbing with surprising ease from a small Austin.

She hurried to the door, opening it as John's mother was transferring a large shopping basket from one hand to the other prior to ringing the bell. Lena Ashley was a tall, raw-boned woman with swept-back greying hair and a face that might have belonged to a man. While her possessiveness had never allowed Sarah to like her, forthrightness and determination had a way of earning their own grudging respect.

"Oh, hello, Mother. Do come in."

A fine drizzle was lying in beads on the woman's hair. Anyone else of her age might have brushed them off, but while Lena Ashley was not above using her health to further her ends, as when she moved houses to Bournemouth, the only indisposition she had known in her life had been during John's birth.

Her voice was in character, low-throated and brisk. "Good morning, dear. I haven't come to stay — only to collect the jumble. Is yours ready yet?"

"Jumble?"

"Yes. Have you forgotten? We've got the Vicar to form an Aid For Refugees Committee and we want all the old clothes we can get. I asked John on Monday evening to mention it to you."

Sarah stood aside for her to enter. "I'm sorry but I haven't heard a thing about it. It must have slipped his mind."

The woman's impatience died at once. "Poor boy. He has so much to think about at work. Has he told you about the big sale he made last week?"

"Yes. It was very good, wasn't it?"

"Wonderful, dear. That huge plot of land that's been lying fallow for all these years. If he goes on like this he's sure to get the area managership when David Reid retires."

No one but John could have made her digress like this, Sarah thought. "Yes, I'm sure he will. Would you like me to go upstairs now and see what old clothes I have?"

"If you please, dear. I've quite a busy morning ahead of me."

Sarah led her upstairs. In her own wardrobe she found three old dresses — two pairs of shoes, and an old nylon mackintosh. From John's tallboy she threw out two shirts, a tie he hated, and three pairs of socks. From the corner of her eye she noticed the careful scrutiny Mrs Ashley gave to each article of John's before stuffing them into her large basket. As Sarah passed her a zip-up cardigan the woman paused.

"You're not going to give this away, are you?"

Sarah turned in surprise. "Yes. Why?

One of the elbows is nearly through and it's starting to fade."

"But it's John's favourite cardigan. The one he always wears for golf."

Tiny, hot needles were suddenly pricking the girl's forehead. "I know that. But he's got another. I wouldn't give this one away if he hadn't."

Lena Ashley laid the cardigan down on the bed. "Just the same, dear, I think I'd rather have his permission before I accept it."

Taking a deep breath the girl closed the tallboy door. "Then that's all I have."

"But what about shoes? I know he has at least two pairs he ought to get rid of. Shoes are the things we need most of all."

"No, I'm sorry. I might really get into trouble if I give his shoes away without permission."

For a moment Lena Ashley's pale blue eyes lifted to her face. In this dimension they were little more than reflective. In another, Sarah thought, they contained seven years of dislike. Then the woman nodded. "Very well, dear. You're probably right. Now I mustn't keep you any longer — I'm sure you have plenty to do."

They walked downstairs. Lena Ashley glanced back. "I was sorry you couldn't come round on Monday evening. Did you finish the dress?"

Sarah nodded. "Almost."

"I must see it some time. I'm sure it looks nice." At the door she held out a cheek for Sarah to kiss. It was a ritual they had long practised: the only doubt in Sarah's mind being who disliked it the most. "Goodbye, dear. We must arrange another evening soon. I'll phone you. Don't forget to give my love to John."

Sarah waited in the porch to wave as the car backed out of the drive. As she withdrew into the house a pang of regret that her own parents were no longer alive made her wince. It was odd, she thought, how at times no one in the world could make one feel lonelier than one's in-laws.

She arrived at the cottage a few minutes before eleven, on Thursday morning. Michael's lack of welcome told her at once he had regretted accepting her offer. As she entered the living room she saw he had been writing — a half-typed sheet of paper was still gripped in the platen of the typewriter.

Careful to keep her eyes away from the typescript she balanced her parcel on the edge of the desk and tore open the paper. Pulling out the books she laid them on the desk. "There you are. One's about writing for television, and the other's about short-story writing. Have you read either of them?"

As he picked up the books she saw his eyes flicker to the carbons and ream of paper still lying in the torn parcel. "No," he muttered. "I haven't seen them before."

"Good. Then they might be some use to you." Encouraged, she turned back to the parcel. "I was wondering if you'd also accept this paper and these few carbons. You must use a lot of paper and I know how expensive it is these days."

His sharp exclamation checked her. His face was suddenly transformed as if the scar, in his spasm of anger, were tugging and distorting the nerves of his eyes and mouth. From passive sullenness he became hostile and quarrelsome.

"You've got a damned nerve — coming here and offering charity like this. Who the hell do you think you are?"

Knowing he had already noticed the ream of paper she was more surprised by his reaction than she would otherwise have been. It was her first experience of the way he sometimes avoided facts related to himself, only to react the more violently when he was brought face to face with them by others.

His thin body took an aggressive step forward. "I noticed your face last week when you first came inside the cottage. You thought it shabby and broken-down, didn't you — a sort of peasant's hovel. And you thought me a tramp in need of charity. Well, you're wrong. I don't need help or any crumbs from a rich woman's table. I thought I'd already told you that."

She lit herself a cigarette. "You're a terribly touchy person, aren't you?"

"Yes. I'm damned touchy when people offer me charity. Because I don't want your help or anyone else's. Now or ever. I just want to be left alone. Is that clear or do I have to spell it out?"

She learned at that moment that no

emotion is as hard to contain as self-righteous anger. "You don't have to spell anything out and you don't need to slap me in the face either. You're the kind of person who makes one say to hell with the world — let it go hungry and let it rot. I'm sorry I wanted to give a hand — I'll even apologise if it'll make you any happier. Now I'm going and don't worry — I shan't make a nuisance of myself again."

She snatched her handbag from a chair and the whole affair might have ended at that moment had there not been a loud knock on the kitchen door. Robbie, lying near the desk, gave a bark and leapt to his feet. A second knock came almost at once, followed by a girl's cheerful voice. "Hello! Is anyone home?"

As Michael started and turned Sarah saw his hand rise involuntarily to his scarred cheek. The dog was now in the kitchen, scratching and barking at the door. The knocking, growing impatient, came for a third time. "Is anyone home? It's the baker here."

Feeling the tension, Sarah moved forward. "Shall I answer it for you?"

He made a jerky, negative gesture and limped into the kitchen. He had trouble with the bolt: it was a few seconds before the door swung open to reveal a handsome, fresh-featured girl in white overalls standing on the step outside. A basket lay at her feet.

"Just in time." Her voice was cheerful again. "I thought you must be out. It's Mr Lindsay, isn't it?"

The way he was standing half-hidden by the door reminded Sarah of his behaviour the night her car broke down. "That's right."

The girl was consulting a pocket book. "I never could make out Dad's handwriting. Is it a small *brown* loaf or a white?"

"A brown." Then, before the girl could speak: "Why hasn't your father come today?"

"Hurt his back," the girl said laconically. "He'll be in plaster another month. So I'm having to do his rounds." Her curious eyes were trying to see round the half-open door. "It's a bit tricky at first, getting to know everyone and what they want."

The sullen man drew farther back into the shadows. The girl reached down into the basket. "A brown — here you are."

Seeing she was holding it out in a way that would force him out into the open, Sarah walked quickly into the kitchen. "Thank you — I'll take it. Good day."

The girl looked both surprised and disappointed. "Oh, hello, Miss. I didn't see you there." To hide her confusion she bent down to pat Robbie who was sniffing around her ankles. "You're a cute little dog, aren't you? I like Scotties. Oh, well; I suppose I'd better be getting along. Cheerio."

He closed the door as if shutting out an enemy and turned sharply away, but not before Sarah saw the traces the encounter had left on his face. Putting the loaf down she returned to the living room. As she stared through the window she knew her own cheeks were pale. That he was sensitive about his appearance she had already known. That he suffered hyperesthesia of this magnitude was a shock that revived all her earlier instincts about him.

It was a full minute before his embarrassment allowed him to follow her. She did not turn — she waited for him to make the first move. She heard the restless shuffle of his footsteps, then his sullen voice.

"I thought you said you were leaving."

She nodded. "I was."

"What do you mean — was? I thought you'd had enough of my ingratitude and bad manners."

She turned sharply. It was a movement that caught him by surprise and what she saw in the unguarded split-second before his mask of defiance dropped back into place vindicated all her instincts. If any human being in the world needed help, it was this lonely, sensitive, self-destructive man. The only doubt left in her was whether she had the courage, the ability, and now the wish to give him that help.

When she did not speak his voice rose and jeered at her. "Well, haven't you? Or are you one of those people who don't know when they've had enough?"

It's going to be hell, she told herself. You'll be a mad fool to attempt it. She

58

took a deep breath, then held out her packet of cigarettes to him.

"I don't know what I am," she said quietly. "Perhaps that's something I'm starting to find out."

5

THE way he took a cigarette made the gesture look punitive. Gazing at his hostile, twisted face, she had an idea. "Will you do me a favour?"

"A favour?" He looked taken aback.

"Yes. I'd like a cup of tea. Will you make me one?"

The innocuity of the request seemed to blunt his hostility. "I suppose so, if that's what you want."

Was this the way to handle him, she wondered, as he withdrew into the kitchen — to make him feel of service? She followed him to the door, trying to lighten her conversation as he filled a kettle over the sink.

"Living on your own like this must have made you self-reliant. Are you a good cook?"

For a moment he did not answer. Then: "I can warm a tin of soup. Or fry sausages and eggs. That about covers it."

"I don't believe you. Men can be excellent cooks."

His footsteps had a hollow ring on the flagstones as he crossed over to the stove. "Some men, maybe. They're usually the ones who care about their bellies."

His occasional use of blunt Anglo-Saxon nouns was something she was to grow accustomed to in the weeks ahead. On this occasion it amused her. "And you don't care about yours that much?"

"Not particularly, no."

He struck a match and applied it to the stove. The jet gave a loud plop and blew itself out. He tried again and this time the gas caught. He set the kettle over it and then turned to her, his expression sardonic.

"You still haven't told me what you think of my hovel. Don't you think it's just the place for a down-and-out scribbler?"

She trod carefully again. "I can see its advantages. It would be hard to find a quieter place."

His laugh was harsh. "You can say that again. If it wasn't for the meter readers you'd be the first person who's been inside it for the last two years."

She stared at him. "You can't be serious!"

He turned and opened the mesh door of the tea chest, clearly regretting his disclosure. She caught a glimpse of the meagre contents before his body screened them: a cracked milk jug, two cups, a few miscellaneous bowls and tins. When he did not answer her curiosity overcame her.

"You can't mean that no-one's visited you the whole time you've been here?"

He put a packet of tea on the top of the chest. "Who'd do the visiting? I've told you — I don't come from these parts."

"But surely you've made some friends in two years?" His glance of dislike was warning she was on thin ice again. "I'm not as keen on people as you seem to be. I can't get far enough away from them."

Seeing there was nothing she could do to help him and uncertain of his mood, she retired into the living room. Although she was still wearing her coat the dankness of the cottage was beginning to chill her and she crossed over to the paraffin heater. As she bent over it she heard his voice.

"What's the matter? Are you cold?"

"It's only my hands," she lied. "I think I must have poor circulation."

When he came in a few minutes later carrying a tray she was examining the photographs of the soldier and the young girl on the chest-of-drawers. She motioned to them as he set the tray down.

"Why is it neither of your two friends here have come to visit you?"

She felt the atmosphere change as his head lifted. She half-expected an explosion but to her relief he recovered himself and gave a harsh laugh. "They'd find it pretty difficult."

"Why is that?"

The desire to punish her was hard in his eyes. "Why? Because they're both dead."

The brutality of the statement shocked her. "Dead! But they're both so young."

"Young people die too. Or didn't you know that?"

He ventured no more information about the young couple and for the next few minutes, while they drank tea and smoked a second cigarette, he hardly spoke a word to her. Already late in leaving for Bere Regis she began wondering what new excuse she could find to see him again. To her relief he provided one as she was stubbing out her cigarette.

"You say you don't mind when you get the books back?"

"No. Keep them as long as you like. But it would be nice to hear you'd found them useful. Might I call round next Thursday to find out?"

For the first time he showed no resistance. "Yes, all right. I'll probably have read them by then."

She left two minutes later. As she reached the car she saw he was again watching her from the cottage step, although the moment she glanced back he withdrew and closed the door. She had a feeling of exhaustion as she sank down into the car seat.

That night, long after John had fallen asleep, she was kept awake by her thoughts. Until today it had been intuition more than knowledge that had made her believe Michael was in need of help, and so an excuse for disentanglement had remained with her. But after what she had seen that day, all her doubts had vanished. If she decided to see no more of him before she was too deeply committed, it would be in the full knowledge she was abandoning a human being who, in his self-destructive bitterness, was perhaps more crippled than if he were locked in the isolated cottage by infirmity.

Already she had the feeling he was beginning to react to her visits: at times his hostility had suggested fear of the need for companionship she was awakening in him again. All her instincts told her his urgent need was for a friend he could talk to, confide in, perhaps even quarrel with. The first vital link to which other links could grow and so rehabilitate him with the world he had withdrawn from. Without it there seemed nothing to stop him becoming further alienated, with consequences her imagination was all too willing to provide.

It was then she had to face the truth she had long avoided — that her marriage gave her no individual freedom whatever in situations of this kind. The affair of

Mr Branson had been a case in point. Branson was a gentle, diffident bachelor in his late forties on the staff of her hairdressers. A year ago, almost by chance, she had discovered he had been tied most of his life to an ailing, widowed mother, and when the old woman had died Sarah had out of pity invited Branson home one evening. It had been a bad mistake: there had been a tepidness in John's manner that a sensitive man like Branson could hardly have missed.

Sympathy had made her suggest another evening, although in her heart she had not relished the ordeal. But when a few days later at Harriet's house John had made a jocular remark about 'Sarah's new boy friend' she had known the impossibility of a second invitation.

She knew that the *avant-garde* would say she was peculiarly unfortunate in her marriage: that in these modern times the restrictions that irked her had in the main been lifted. The women novelists proclaimed the new freedoms almost hysterically, as did the playwrights of the theatre and television. Intellectuals could be such fools, she thought. A few weeks in the provinces or even outside their own set in London, and they would learn that for ninety per cent of the married population nothing had changed at all. Tolerance was something one gave to the other man or woman, never to ones husband or wife. She saw it in the marriages of her friends and now, distressingly because of her affection for John, she recognized it in her own. And knew that the restlessness that had troubled her over the last year was a part of the same claustrophobic syndrome.

This admission about her marriage tended for a while to over-shadow her concern for Michael, and she tried to deceive herself that if the situation were put squarely to John he would not place obstacles in her way. Basically he was a kind man and no-one could know Michael without being aware of some need in him, whatever the interpretation of that need might be.

But to know Michael one had to meet him — John, she knew, would insist on it — and once again every instinct told her such a meeting would be a disaster. The two men could hardly be more different in ideas and temperament and it would not need John, who would be utterly at sea with Michael, to lose his patience first. No matter how a confrontation between the two men was contrived, it seemed beyond doubt that the fiercest hostility would come from the hypersensitive Michael. Whatever John's reactions to him — even if wholly tolerant — it would clearly become impractical, if not impossible, for her to continue paying lone visits to the cottage.

One human being offering a hand to another — that was the heart of the matter because in loneliness a man found solace from one person and not from many. In other words, whatever John's character, the situation demanded that she met Michael alone until a break-through were achieved. And with John the man he was, the risks of secret visits were great and self-interest told her she would be a fool to take them.

Yet one thought kept coming to her. Of all the hundreds and thousands of cars that must have passed Michael's cottage over the years, hers had been the one to break down and she the one to seek his help. Moreover, his aggressive, self-destructive behaviour had not turned her against him, which for one as quick-tempered and easily hurt as she, was the most puzzling feature of all. It was not difficult for her, lying there in the darkness, to think their encounter might have been more than chance.

The realist in her came to the rescue. She was melodramatizing the affair in every possible way and hurrying a decision that need not yet be made. She could call on Michael a couple more times yet — perhaps even take him a food parcel — without doing him any harm and without committing herself. After that, if she saw danger signs looming ahead, she could always find an excuse for curtailing her visits.

Comforted by this procrastination she was able to close her eyes at last and let the demands of sleep have their way.

6

IT took her two more visits to the cottage before she made the breakthrough that was to change her relationship with Michael. It happened three days before Christmas when, without warning, she arrived just before noon. She had brought with her some groceries and two tins of paraffin, but with no idea how to present them she left them for the moment in the car.

"Hello," she smiled as he opened the door. "I hope you don't mind my surprising you like this. But because of Christmas I've had to change my visiting day this week."

"No, that's all right," he muttered. "Come in."

In the narrow passage she ran into Robbie's frenzied welcome. She laughed as she patted him. "I think he sees me as an endless bar of chocolate."

The living room was in some disorder: the chairs were pulled aside, the carpet rolled back, and a sweeping brush rested against the bookcase.

"What's this?" she asked, amused. "Your day for housework?"

He nodded. "I usually do it on Mondays. Then I've the rest of the week free."

She thought how thin and pale he looked in his ragged pullover. "It's almost lunch time. What are you having today?"

"I don't know. An egg, I suppose."

"You need more than an egg, particularly in this weather." Hesitating, she took her courage in both hands. "Look, will you do me a favour? For Christmas?"

He was on his guard instantly. "What do you mean — for Christmas?"

"Never mind. First you have to promise not to be angry at what I'm going to ask you."

He hesitated. Then, impatiently: "Oh, all right. What is it?"

She went to the door. "Wait here. I won't be a moment." Running out to the car she returned with the shopping bag of groceries. "I didn't arrange to have lunch with my friend today; I thought that perhaps you'd let me have it here instead. So I've brought these few things along."

His face had set hard at the sight of the shopping bag. Knowing it was going to be touch and go she moved towards him. "Don't forget your promise. In any case, if you think about it, there's no cause to lose your temper."

His effort at self-control made his voice gritty. "I've told you a dozen times — I hate charity."

"Who's giving charity? I've brought these things because I want a meal myself."

"Oh, for God's sake, why lie about it? You think I'm broke and need my belly filling. So why not say so?"

For a moment she allowed her own temper to slip. "What if I do? Is it such a sin at Christmas time? Why can't you put your pride in your pocket for once and let someone else be happy?"

The gamble worked. He stared at her aggressively, then suddenly turned away. "All right. If you want to be a fool and waste your money, why should I mind?"

He moved over to the desk where he played moodily with the keys of his typewriter. She gave him a moment, then asked quietly. "Do you like pork sausages?"

"Yes, I suppose so."

"Good. Then we'll have sausages, peas, and chips — they won't take long to do. If you'll lend me a frying pan and something to warm the peas in, I'll get started."

Anticipating resistance all along the line she had brought cooking fat and a few potatoes with her. But after she removed her coat he followed her into the kitchen and opened up the tea chest. After putting the utensils she needed on the stove he withdrew again into the living room.

When she had cut up the chips she was forced to call him back again. "I wonder if you'd mind lighting the gas for me. I noticed it back-fires unless you do it the right way."

He lit the jets she indicated, then moved moodily to one side. Winning his confidence, she thought ruefully, was like chipping away rust, flake by painful flake. She dropped the fat into the pan and then turned to him.

"What are you working on at the moment?"

"A short story," he muttered.

"Is that what you write — short stories?"

"Mostly."

"Then you do write other things too?"

"I do a bit on a novel now and then. But it'll be months before it's finished."

She dropped the chips into the pan. "What was your last short story called?"

"'Erosion'."

"Have you sent it to a magazine yet?"

"Yes. Weeks ago."

"Are you happy with it?"

"Not particularly." He moved towards the living room.

"I've a letter to finish. It has to go off today."

She was not sorry to be left alone: the strain of making conversation was beginning to tell on her. She took the two plates he had given her and opened the oven door, wondering if she dared apply a match to the sinister row of jets inside. Her courage failed and she laid the plates beneath the grill instead. When all was prepared she gave him a call.

"Lunch is ready. If you wouldn't mind clearing the table I'll bring it through."

She noticed he did not sit down until she was seated herself. There was a frown on his scarred face as if the sight of so much food had a hypnotic effect on him. At first he ate hesitantly, but her small talk helped to put him at ease, and by the time the meal was over he had new colour in his cheeks.

She brought coffee in and then gave him a cigarette. "Well," she said, sitting back. "Wasn't that better than just a boiled egg?"

The wry twist of his lips was almost the first smile she had received from him. "A little, yes."

She thought how much better looking he appeared and realized, with a sense of eeriness, that the reason lay in the scar. Like a living thing that had been subdued it had become a mere puckered line down his cheek, with all its influence over his expression removed.

A silence followed in which she could suddenly find nothing to say. She knew she must not look at him and yet when he leaned down to pat the dog her eyes were drawn back to the scar as if it were a magnet. It's whole effect on his appearance was psychological, she realized. In moments such as this, when the stress had gone from him, he was a normal, good-looking man.

His changed voice made her start. "You can't keep your eyes off it, can you? What's the matter — haven't you seen a freak before?"

She felt hot and cold with horror. "What are you talking about?"

His hand rose to the scar, a gesture of aversion. "I've noticed how you watch me. You're dying to know how I got this and my smashed-up leg, aren't you?"

She half-rose from her chair in panic. "I don't want to know anything. Don't quarrel with me today, please. Not with Christmas so close."

Perverse as he was in his bitterness, she could have said nothing more guaranteed to make him talk. The scar was crawling back and changing his expression. "What's the matter? Don't you like anything but fairy stories at Christmas time?"

"It's not that. I don't want you to hurt yourself."

"Hurt myself. By talking about it?" His laugh made her flinch. "Christ, you don't understand much, do you?"

It was then she knew what the moment signified. "I'm sorry," she said quietly, sinking back into her chair. "I'd be glad to hear it if you care to tell me."

"You're sure? It's not pretty. It's not something that's going to brighten your day."

"I don't expect it to." She glanced at the two photographs. "You did tell me they were both dead."

His hostility seemed to diminish as he followed her gaze to the chest-of-drawers. "You've guessed something of it then?"

"Not really. It just seemed likely they might be involved."

"Not both of them," he muttered. "Only the soldier. His name was David Adams — we were in the same class at school and grew up together. About the only thing we couldn't see eye to eye on was what we wanted to be. Dave fancied the Army and I hated the idea. So when we left school we parted ways for a time. He joined up and I stayed in Doncaster and got a job in a small engineering firm."

She sat very still, afraid of breaking the tenuous thread of confidence. He patted the restless dog again before continuing.

"Apart from a short leave Dave was away quite a time. He did a spell in Singapore and was then sent to Hong Kong. But when he got back they gave him a staff job in a camp near Leeds and we started seeing one another again. He married a Doncaster girl and the four of us used to visit one another on alternate weekends."

She wondered who the fourth person of the quartet would be. His girl friend? Or had he also married by this time?

"Dave and I were keen on soccer in those days and used to follow Leeds United. Sometimes we'd go on excursions when they were playing away from home. One Saturday we went to Liverpool and after the match thought we'd take a look round the town. About seven it started to rain and we went into a pub in the dock area. We left it late to catch the train and took a short cut across some waste land. It was as dark as hell and halfway across we ran into half a dozen teenagers beating up two coloured men. One of them was on the ground and looked in a bad way, and Dave went straight in. I'm not much good at that sort of thing myself but there wasn't much I could do but follow him.

"Dave was pretty useful with his fists and knocked two of them down. The others left the coloured men and went for him. They dragged him down and started putting the boot in. When I tried to help, one of them came at me with a flick knife."

He drew smoke into his lungs. "I could hear them kicking Dave but all I could see was the knife and this teenager's face. His lips were bleeding where Dave had hit him and he was snarling like an animal. I was too scared to know what was happening when suddenly they all ran into an alley and a truck engine started up — I thought they were running away and bent over Dave to see how he was. The next minute headlights swung on us and started getting bigger and bigger."

Her mouth was dry with tension. "You're not saying they ran you down?"

He nodded. "They came straight at us

and all I could do was crouch there like some paralyzed rabbit. I don't remember much about it — that's half the trouble. All at once I found myself lying on the road, with my face numb and wet and unable to move my leg. There wasn't any pain. The truck had vanished and Dave was about six yards away, all twisted up."

He drew on his cigarette again. "I couldn't call out to him — it felt as if the whole side of my face had gone. But I knew the two men we'd tried to help must have seen it happen and would fetch help." His laugh was like the grate of metal. "You see what a simple kid I was in those days — I really believed people did things like that."

"You mean they didn't help you?"

"Of course they didn't. It was attempted murder and they didn't want to get mixed up in it. Who does want to get mixed up in anything unpleasant? That's people. That's life. Only I was too naïve to know it."

It was not easy to speak. "How long was it before you were found?"

"A hell of a time. At least it seemed to

80

be. They said later it was the delay that cost Dave his life. He had an internal haemorrhage and it had gone on too long."

"What about you?"

"I'd eight months in hospital. I'd two fractures of the femur and a broken hip. I'd also this — " he touched his cheek, a gesture of revulsion " — and plenty of time to think."

She wondered what one could say that would not sound impossibly false or banal. He appeared to read her mind.

"Oh, I don't mean about the teenagers and the coloured men. You only need one experience like that to show you what an innocent fool you've been. But it's not so easy to face the truth about yourself."

"What do you mean by that?"

He gave her a look of dislike. "You haven't much imagination, have you? I said I was leaning over Dave when the truck came at us. Then how did I end up five or six yards away with only a broken leg and messed-up face when the wheels had gone right over him?"

She stiffened. "That's ridiculous. Anything can happen when a vehicle hits two people. It probably caught you a glancing blow and threw you sideways."

"It could also have hit me as I was starting to run away, couldn't it?" he sneered. "Or even swung round and caught me up. I was far enough away."

"This is all in your mind. You're a sensitive person and you felt guilty because Dave was dead and you survived. So you've blamed yourself for it. I don't for a moment believe you ran away. In any case, you couldn't have saved him."

His hand savagely crushed the stub of cigarette into an ashtray. "I could have tried, couldn't I?"

"Perhaps you did try. You said you couldn't remember anything. But I still don't see that it matters." Then she gave a start. "Unless his wife put the idea into your head. Did she?"

He ignored the direct question. "Every time she and Judy used to visit me I'd think that if I'd kept my head and dragged him to one side they might have gone straight past and not come back."

"You're too sensitive," she said again. "The thought probably never entered her head. Tell me about Judy. Was she your wife?" When he gave a start but did not answer she trod with infinite care. "I'm sorry. If you'd rather not talk about her I'll understand."

He had not missed her glance at the girl in the photograph and his hard laugh jarred her. "So that's it? You think she's dead. That's damned funny. People like Judy don't die — didn't you know that? They get rich and live for ever."

She realized with a shock what deep water she was in. His voice was now a whip striking her. "You love jumping to conclusions, don't you? I wouldn't have a photograph of that bitch inside the cottage if someone paid me ten thousand a year for it. I've enough to remind me what life's all about without her face sneering at me all day long."

A chill ran through her as she began to understand. "Don't talk about that now. Tell me some other time."

"What's the matter?" he jeered. "Don't you want to hear the truth about your sex? Yes, she was my wife. We'd been married for two years. In church, with all the trimmings. For richer and poorer, in sickness and in health — all the usual jazz. And I took in every damned word of it at the time."

The dog whined and drew closer to him. His bleak eyes stared down at it, then rose again to her face. "She fooled me completely those first two years. If another girl as much as looked at me there was hell to pay. I thought that was love, as most other people do. Christ, what a shock I had coming."

As he paused she felt the tension in her throat again. "It was like that until the day of the accident. Then it all changed. At first I thought it was only shock. Then I began to notice the way she looked at me after the bandages were taken off. I'd tell her not to worry, that it wasn't too bad and I could live with it, and she'd give a tight nod and talk about something else. Then she began paying fewer visits to the hospital. At first she'd miss only one night and she'd always have a good excuse. Then it would be two and three times a week. And when she came she gave me the feeling she was in a hurry to get away. I couldn't blame her — eight months is a hell of a long time to visit a hospital and she was having to work full-time to keep the hire-purchase payments going. I tried to get my discharge but my hip hadn't set properly and I still couldn't walk.

"The thing blew up when I got home. Before the accident she'd hardly let me out of her sight — now she'd made new friends and was out with them nearly every evening. I was a little time working it out but then I got the message. She'd grabbed me like all women grab men — because you've all been brainwashed into thinking you haven't made it until you're married. You must have your own home to show off to your friends: you must have kids before you're fulfilled as women. The system tells you you must, and so do the ads. The man — he's the status-symbol and who cares what status-symbols feel as long as they dish out the sex and the money?"

His bitterness made her close her eyes.

"Yes, I got the message all right. That was why she used to hang on to me like that. I was her most precious possession — she could show me off to her friends like a shiny new car. But not any longer. No-one was going to get jealous over the Michael Mark II with a smashed-in radiator and broken suspension. All I was likely to raise was a titter, and there's no fun in that for any girl. So one day she walked out with the chap she'd been having an affair with and the party was over."

She cleared her throat. "Is that when you came down here?"

"Right. I couldn't get out of the place fast enough. She's made me insure myself and with that and the money I got for the furniture I was able to buy this cottage." He stared bitterly round the room. "The old boy who lived here was itching to get out. I know he did me with the price but who cared — it was what I wanted."

She knew he meant the isolation. His paroxysm of bitterness appeared to have burned out and his grimace was almost apologetic as he accepted a cigarette from her. "All right — now you've heard it. And a load of self-pity it must have sounded. But don't blame me — you asked for it."

"I'm not blaming you. I'm glad you told me."

"Glad? That's funny." He took a light from her, then gave his hard laugh. "What are you thinking? That I'm the sourest man you've ever met?"

"If you were, it wouldn't be your fault. But I wasn't thinking that at all."

"Then what were you thinking?"

"I was wondering who the girl in the photograph was if she wasn't your wife."

"My sister," he muttered. "She died a couple of years ago, just before I came down here. No one knew the reason — it was some damned virus or other."

She shook her head in disbelief. His tone changed immediately as he saw her expression. "Don't start feeling sorry for me. You've done well so far — don't spoil it now."

"I'm not feeling sorry for you. But you have had atrocious luck, haven't you — particularly with your marriage?"

He gave a cynical shrug. "Have I? Who's to say? Perhaps it's those who have to sweat it out you should feel sorry for."

It was a remark that seemed to sum up his distrust of people, particularly women. Certain he would soon regret his confidences and punish her for listening to them, she tried to get him talking about his work.

"Have you heard anything yet from the magazine you sent your last story to? The one you called 'Erosion'."

"Yes, I've heard," he muttered. "They returned it two days ago."

"What did they say about it?"

"Say! They don't say anything. They send you a bloody rejection slip and that's it."

His increasing hostility was her warning and she took it. "Eunice expects me around two o'clock, so I suppose I must think about leaving. What about the dishes? Do you mind if I leave them for you to wash?"

"Why should I mind? I'm not in demand like you are — I've all the time in the world."

She put on her coat and went over to her shopping basket, hoping she had not left it too late. Without looking at him she began putting the contents on the desk. "I'm leaving these few things here, Michael. Please use them up over Christmas."

His exclamation made the dog start. "You keep at it, don't you? On and on and on."

"And you won't pocket your pride, will you? Not even at Christmas time."

He turned away but not before she saw the blcakness of his eyes. "What's Christmas to do with it? It's only another day, like all the others."

Her mind had been avoiding it but now it was all there: the windswept heath, the lonely, brooding cottage. "No, it's not just another day. If I could possibly manage it I'd come to visit you. As I can't, I want you to accept these few things — they might help just a little."

"Help who? You?"

She winced. "Yes. It's I who wants it, I suppose."

He stared at her, then his gaze dropped. "I'm sorry," he muttered. "I know I'm an ungrateful bastard. All right — leave them if you want to."

There was a new bitterness about him that she was sensitive enough to interpret. "You could give me something for Christmas too, if you felt like it."

"You must be joking. What have I to give you?"

"You could lend me a copy of that short story — the one the magazine has just returned. Please," she said quickly before he had time to refuse. "I really would like to read it. And then when I come again we could talk about it. Won't you do that for me?"

A full fifteen seconds must have passed before he moved reluctantly towards the desk. "You won't like it — I'm sure of that."

She had a feeling of success as he pulled a thin manuscript from a drawer and thrust it at her. "Thank you. I shall read it over Christmas."

At the front door she paused and turned to him. "Are you certain you're going to be all right?"

Her departure had changed his mood again and his laugh mocked her. "What's the matter? Are you worried about me?"

"It's not a matter of being worried. I don't like the idea of your being alone over Christmas."

Was it her imagination or was his silence a challenge? *If Christmas means so much to you, then why don't you invite me round to your home? I might throw the offer back into your face but at least it would prove you aren't a hypocrite.*

A lie seemed her only escape. "We're going away for Christmas or you could have spent an evening with us."

The scar disfigured his face as he laughed. "Me! Among your wealthy relatives and friends — with my elbows sticking out of my pullover! I can just see your husband going along with that."

The attack on John made her turn quickly away. "I'll have to go now. But I'll come round in the morning next week so we'll have plenty of time to talk."

As she reached her car she remembered the two tins of paraffin in the boot. She hesitated, then shook her head. To ask him to swallow his pride twice in one day was to ask too much. It was enough he had accepted one gift from her and in return given her his confidence. Perhaps it was more than enough, for it surely meant she was committed.

7

SHE read Michael's short story, 'Erosion', the following morning after John had gone to work. It was about a young teacher who was persuaded by his pretty, money-conscious wife into accepting a job in the advertising world. Quickly disgusted by the jungle in which he found himself he longed to escape, but he was now deep in hire-purchase debts and a return to teaching would mean losing the possessions his wife valued so much. After much soul-searching he decided to endure the work for three more years when his new possessions would be paid for and he could return to teaching again.

The three years passed and brought the twist-end to the story. Corrupted now by the jungle he once hated, the man could no longer stomach the reduction in living standards that school teaching would bring. Now it was his wife, frightened by the change in him, who vainly urged him to go back.

It was a story whose moral point could hardly fail to move Sarah in her present critical mood towards society. Her discovery that Michael, beneath his self-destructive exterior, had such thoughts fascinated her and made it difficult for her to judge the story as a piece of literature.

The Christmas holidays arrived. John closed his branch office after lunch on Wednesday and arrived home early after a staff party. She was in the living room when his car entered the drive and she heard him run up the steps to the side door. Guessing his condition as she heard him humming, she went into the hall to greet him. As he saw her his hand went guiltily behind his back.

"Hello," she smiled. "I didn't expect you home so early. Wasn't the party much fun?"

His fresh-complexioned face was flushed and he looked self-conscious: in John a sign of intoxication. "No, the party was all right. I left before it ended, that's all."

"But why? There was no need to. I

didn't expect you back before six at the earliest."

He looked like a well-intentioned, embarrassed schoolboy standing there at the door. "I had a few drinks and then felt like getting back to you. So I said goodbye and came."

This was one of the things about John she loved. Some men became morose after a few drinks, some turned sexual, some wanted to fight. John became sentimental, sometimes absurdly but always endearingly.

"That was sweet of you, darling. And I'm very happy to see you."

Looking pleased, and unable to keep his secret any longer, he whisked a large spray of flowers from behind his back and held them out to her. They were red carnations and there was a stinging in her eyes as she took them: red carnations were her favourite flowers.

"Darling, they're beautiful. How sweet of you."

"Do you like them?"

"You know I do." Reaching up, she kissed him. "Thank you very much."

He would not release her, kissing her

again and again. Then he rubbed his cheek against her hair. "We are good friends again, aren't we?" he muttered.

She glanced quickly up at him. "What on earth do you mean?"

He avoided her eyes by drawing her close again. "I thought we'd been a bit touchy with one another recently. There isn't anything wrong, is there, darling?"

Her laugh caught in her throat at his tone. Gripping his arm she pressed against him. "Of course there isn't. Don't be so silly."

"Are you sure? Honestly?"

"Of course I'm sure."

He gave a sigh of relief. "Thank goodness for that." He lowered his voice: he was still English in spite of his semi-intoxication. "Because I love you. You know that, don't you, darling?"

As his arms tightened around her again, the smell of the carnations rose to her nostrils. Carnations always took her back to their courtship and the early days of their marriage. Before John had moved to Marks & Marks and when real estate had meant no more to either of them than a cottage in the country and the welcoming bark of a dog on their return home.

The yearning to escape back and begin again was almost a pain at that moment. At the same time an inner, realistic voice was chiding her for her romanticism. To each his own nature: John liked, perhaps needed, the ruthless cut and thrust of business and the symbols of success that it brought. And who was she to be so certain of happiness without the security and the possessions that other women cherished?

Yet with the red carnations pouring their scent into her mind it was easy to be as sentimental as he at that moment. "I know, darling," she whispered, pressing harder against him. "And I love you too. Very, very much."

Over Christmas, as always, John was generous to her, giving her money to buy a new dress and presenting her on Christmas morning with an expensive marcasite brooch. They spent the afternoon and evening with his mother and on Boxing Day went out with Harriet and Robert and two other friends to a pub in the New Forest. Everyone was in excellent humour — even Harriet appeared to have declared a truce with Robert over the Nativity — and that night (as if — and Sarah's amused thought was entirely affectionate — to celebrate the holiday's successful conclusion) John made love to her.

At her first opportunity she paid a visit to the public library where, after seeking advice from the librarian, she took home two books devoted to the modern short story and its markets. She had decided she could hardly criticize Michael's work without some slight technical knowledge. She also felt that to possess it would help further his confidence in her.

She read the books and then his short story again. This time she found defects. He used too many adjectives and in moments of emotion his vocabulary seemed to lack depth. He was inclined to lecture his moral points and to use too much narrative in the process. Yet in spite of this there was a certain power in the story that made her keenly anticipate her visit that week.

At first his behaviour puzzled her. At the door of the cottage his greeting was almost eager and yet she had no sooner removed her coat and entered the living room than he became fidgety and excessively sullen.

"I hope you didn't come specially today," he muttered. "You didn't need to, you know."

Seeing his eyes touch her handbag and then move sharply away, she understood. Every writer, every artist, needed an audience, yet for years he had written to an empty room. Now that she had come along and expressed interest, his need for her opinion was both a hunger and a thirst.

She took the manuscript from her bag. "That's where you're wrong. I've been longing to talk to you about this story."

The sight of the manuscript seemed to unnerve him: he moved to the desk and picked up a book. He flicked over the pages for a moment, then glanced over his shoulder. "Well, what did you think? Was it too awful?"

Whatever her views might have been, she knew his behaviour would have driven her into a white lie. "You know perfectly well it isn't. I enjoyed it very much."

He gave her a suspicious glance before

turning back to the book.

"The idea's excellent," she went on. "Cut-throat business does affect some people that way."

"What about the characters?" he muttered. "Were they all right?"

"Yes. Very realistic." She feigned impatience. "For heaven's sake stop looking at that book and let's talk about it. I'm interested even if you're not."

She could have said nothing better to convince him of her sincerity or to help him overcome his diffidence. As he dropped into a chair she offered him a cigarette to relax him further.

"How many short stories have you written so far?"

"I'm not sure. About twenty, I think."

"How many have you sold?"

He laughed. "Two."

"Stories like this one?"

"Good God, no. Magazines don't take anything like that these days. No, they were a couple of love stories. And I'd go up the wall if I kept on writing stuff like that day after day."

Her feminine streak of practicality was at work, arguing that first things came first and his urgent need was to make some money.

"I can see that, but if there isn't much chance of selling more serious work until you're better known, isn't it wiser to write lighter things first and work your way up?"

Her logic made him frown. "To me most of the stuff's damned immoral — brain-washing kids into thinking they've only to fall in love and get married and their troubles are over. Literature ought to prepare them for life, not feed them a pack of sentimental lies."

To her surprise she found herself half-agreeing with him. "Then what about a good thriller? Entertainment whose deceptions can't do much harm. Entertainment's very important you know. It can help a lot of people to forget their troubles for a time."

She saw his eyes move for a moment to the photograph of his sister. Bitter and intense as he was, she half-expected a didactic lecture on the duties of a writer. Instead he eyed her with new respect.

"I suppose you're right. It certainly seemed to work that way with my sister."

"Your sister?"

"She was bed-ridden for the last couple of months and read every light novel and magazine story she could lay her hands on."

She dared not offer him sympathy. "Was she living with your parents?"

"No. They separated when we were kids and both got married again. An old spinster aunt brought us up."

She had often wondered about his family background. "So you lived with your aunt and sister until you were married?"

His eyes seemed drawn back to the photograph. "I hadn't much choice. The old girl was getting on a bit then and Joan felt we ought to pay her back for what she'd done for us. She always did think of people that way." He turned back to her with a hard laugh. "I'd say that's why she was killed off, wouldn't you?"

The comment made her wince and change the subject. As his mood lightened again his long-frustrated need to talk about his work betrayed itself, and he said enough to make her realize the diversity and originality of his thinking. It was

101

her first contact with a working-class radical, and finding some of his ideas anti-social she tended to attribute them to his adverse background. Nevertheless she felt a sense of discovery listening to him, and when she rose it was with regret.

"I'll have to go, Michael, or Eunice will give me up. But I've enjoyed the talk. Have you another story I can read?"

He glanced at the desk. "This one isn't finished yet."

"Then what about an earlier one?"

"I'd rather give you something new. In any case, they're all packed away upstairs and might take a bit of finding."

Late as she was, she did not press him. "All right, if you promise to let me read the one you're working on now. I take it I can come round again next week?"

"Yes, if you want to. Unless you'd rather — " He paused and made a gesture of impatience. "No, it's stupid. Forget it."

She made him face her. "What were you going to ask me?"

"I wondered if you could come round one evening instead of during the day.

When I'm working time doesn't drag too much, but the evenings can be a bit grim. But it was a daft idea — I know you can't make it."

The cottage suddenly seemed to have gone very quiet. She felt that if she refused this, his first request, he would not hold out his hand to her again.

"It's possible I might be able to arrange it," she said, wondering if she were procrastinating again or telling the truth. "I'll try for next Wednesday evening and let you know. I can write you here, I suppose?"

"Yes. Heath Cottage, Foresters Lane. There's one post, in the morning."

She nodded without meeting his eyes. "All right. I'll let you know before the weekend. I promise to do my best."

The opportunity to speak to John came that evening when she joined him in the sitting room after dinner. He was watching television; as she approached the settee he turned towards her.

"I forgot to tell you, darling — Mother phoned me at the office today. She'd like us to go round next week and I suggested

Thursday. Is that all right?"

"Yes, I suppose so. We've nothing on."

He nodded, his eyes drawn back to the screen as a bevy of scantily-dressed, slim-hipped girls danced into view. She knew she would not get a better time to ask him and yet found herself hesitating: his passion for 'togetherness' never made it easy to obtain an evening for herself. And the knowledge she had to tell him a lie added to her diffidence.

Yet the cottage on the heath had never been more in her thoughts. Listening to the expensive television set she thought of the asthmatic old radio to which Michael was probably listening. With the darkness outside pressing against the dank walls, the winter nights would seem endless.

She took a deep breath. "While we're talking about next week, Eunice asked me today if I could possibly spend a few evenings with her. Her husband looks like being away for a long time yet — he's working on a big building scheme in Manchester — and she gets very depressed if she's left alone too long."

The sudden, indefinable hardening of his expression was something she had never grown accustomed to. "That chap always seems to be away. Why don't the two of them go and live in Manchester and have done with it?"

"What good would that do? He might be sent to Scotland or Cornwall the next time."

"Isn't there any provision for wives to go along with them?"

"Obviously there can't be. In any case, how could they afford to keep moving their furniture about?"

He shrugged. "Moral — don't marry an engineer."

He never changes, she thought. He resents Eunice and Maurice because they are my personal friends, and so he is forcing me to make the pace. Her voice was tarter than she had intended.

"It wasn't the advantage or otherwise of marrying engineers I was talking about. It's whether you mind getting your own dinner on Wednesday evenings. That's all I want — one evening a week."

He turned back to the television set. "Don't worry about me. I'll manage."

"There won't be very much to manage. I shall leave everything ready — all you'll have to do is warm the meal up."

He nodded moodily, then glanced back at her. "What time are you thinking of getting home these nights?"

"It's a little difficult to say. But I should be back before you go to bed. Eleven or eleven-thirty, I suppose."

"I don't like you driving about at that time," he muttered. "The roads out there can be tricky at this time of the year."

Knowing there was now genuine concern behind his sulkiness she managed a smile. "Don't worry — I'll drive carefully."

She soon realized, with dismay, it was not the only deception she had to practise — the possibility existed that John might try to phone her one Wednesday evening. Her first thought was that she must tell Eunice everything. But with the honeymoon shine still on her, Eunice could be conventional herself about how married people should conduct themselves, and although she could be trusted with a secret it seemed unfair to ask for her protection in this instance. After much heart-searching Sarah decided the only answer was to cover one fable with another.

She wrote Michael before the weekend, telling him she could come round on Wednesday evening for dinner. When Wednesday came she left home immediately after lunch and drove straight to Bere Regis. Unhappy at her deception she postponed making it until tea time.

"Do you remember my telling you about that old school teacher of mine who came down to live in Bournemouth a couple of years ago," she said as Eunice passed her a second cup of tea. "I called round to see her the other day and got quite a shock — she's had a stroke that's paralysed one side of her face."

Across the table Eunice was showing appropriate signs of sympathy. I'm telling this like a practised liar, Sarah thought, her hands damp with self-disgust.

"Poor old thing," Eunice said. "Why don't you bring her with you sometime? It would be a change for her."

She made herself continue. "That's the problem. She always was a shy person and now, with this disfigurement, she hates meeting people and will hardly go out of the house. She's so lonely I promised to go round occasionally in the evenings — perhaps on my way back home after seeing you. But I can't tell John about her — he'd want to go with me — so I've had to tell him a small fib. I hope you don't mind."

A small cloud of uneasiness appeared in Eunice's eyes. "Fib? But why?"

"I know it sounds stupid but if I didn't take John with me he'd get all sulky and offended. And if I did take him it would upset her and she wouldn't trust me again."

"Are you sure he wouldn't understand?" the girl asked. "I'm sure Maurice would, once I'd explained everything to him."

Her feeling of guilt made her quick to critize. Why did women make their husbands sound such paragons if you gave them the slightest excuse for thinking yours was below par? Now she found herself defending John.

"John wouldn't stop me seeing her but he'd want to be in on the act, and I've just explained why that wouldn't work. So I've had to tell him I might spend a few Wednesday evenings here with you.

I'm not asking you to tell any lies for me," she went on quickly as Eunice's mouth opened. "All you need to do if he ever phones is to say I've left early that particular evening. And not let on I haven't spent other Wednesday evenings with you."

Eunice's freckled forehead looked warm as she pushed a brown curl back from it. Watching her, Sarah found herself growing irritable.

"You don't need to feel guilty about it. I'm not doing anything wrong."

"You know I wasn't thinking that," the girl protested. "It's just that I don't want to do anything that might come between you and John."

"You won't be coming between anybody. All you'll be doing is helping me give a little time to somebody who desparately needs it. That isn't so terrible, is it?"

Eunice's face cleared. "Of course it isn't. Don't worry. I won't give you away."

Although nothing more was said, she was still filled with self-disgust and resentment when she left Eunice half an hour later. Nothing that had happened to her yet seemed to emphasize more the restrictions she chafed under than this need to lie to and embarrass a friend. At the same time she could not suppress twinges of alarm. From the way deception apparently led to deception, the consequences could be out of proportion to the deed unless she took the greatest care in the future. It was a prospect that at the moment seemed both disagreeable and intimidating.

8

WITH John believing she was with Eunice on Wednesdays, Sarah began her weekly evening visits to Michael's cottage. For the first month her procedure was to have an early dinner with the girl before leaving. Then, feeling it was her one opportunity to ensure Michael had a substantial meal, she began to leave around 5:30 and cooked him a meal on her arrival.

Three months passed and the long winter nights began to shorten into spring. By this time the improvement in Michael was marked: he now looked forward to her visits with an eagerness that at times worried her. Her concern for his welfare no longer roused in him the same resentment and towards the end of March — although not without a great deal of self-examination — he even accepted a second-hand transistor radio she had picked up cheaply.

But she still found it desperately

difficult to help him with the basic necessities of living. Food he would accept from her only when she shared it with him: money never. And there was every sign his financial situation was growing desperate. While he had taken her advice and was now writing light stories for women's magazines, he had made no sale since meeting her, and she knew his mortgage payments had eaten up most of his small insurance compensation.

The crisis came in May when she arrived one evening to find the electricity supply had been cut off. Forcing a confession from him she discovered he owed money to all the essential services and most of the local tradesmen, and all were now demanding payment.

His relapse into his old bitterness was something she understood: he was secretly terrified he might be evicted and forced into contact with the outside world again. In this area — his psychological sensitivity over his appearance and his abdication from society — she had made no progress at all. Apart from herself, the only other person he would voluntarily face was an old hedge trimmer who occasionally called at the cottage for a cup of tea. In spite of her visits he still lived a desperately lonely life and she knew her task would not have begun until he was persuaded to mix with people again.

First, however, she had to make certain he was not evicted. Her efforts to help him were stormy — at one point she was ordered out of the cottage — but in the end, by insisting she was only offering a loan and would expect payment the moment he made a sale, she succeeded in lending him enough money to pay the bills. The total was the not inconsiderable one of twenty-four pounds, and to raise it she had to draw on a small personal legacy left her by her father. Nevertheless it was, as she was fully aware, a victory that would have been inconceivable three months ago.

But the problem of getting him to venture from the cottage and to make social contacts remained. Now that the traffic down the lane was increasing with the advent of summer he had even stopped using it for his daily walk with the dog and was taking footpaths across the heath instead. Conscious a way had to be found of breaking down his resistance, she was brought face to face with a personal problem. Wareham was only fifteen miles from Bournemouth and many of the beauty spots of the district — Lulworth Cove, Corfe Castle, St Albans Head, Chapmans Pool — were in its vicinity. She knew, moreover, the local pubs were also attractive and in the spring and summer many of her friends enjoyed a run out to one after a hot day in the office.

She kept on trying to rationalize her fears, arguing that if the worst happened and she were seen with Michael, no great harm would come of it. John would not like the lies she had told him but once her explanation was made he would accept she was not having an affair. She would almost convince herself until a vision of Harriet, curled up like a kitten in an armchair, would appear and send a thrill of alarm through her.

With the evenings lengthening, even her car outside the cottage became a problem. During the summer the lane was used as a diversion to filter traffic from the congested Wareham road and there was always the danger the car might be seen and recognized.

She overcame the latter problem by asking Michael to clear the path and draw aside the broken gate. "If you'll do that I think I'll be able to get the car into the front garden. I ought to try now that the traffic's getting heavier — there's always the chance that some idiot might run into it."

She was afraid to tell him the real reason in case it brought a return of tension into their relationship. The few times she had mentioned John he had shown hostility and it was not likely to diminish if he knew of the artifices necessary to see him.

Her first real attempt to draw him away from the cottage was made the third week in May. It was a sunny evening and they were out in the back garden, she in a deck chair, he lying supine on a rug. Larks were rising from the open heath and blossom was white on the apple trees. He was wearing an open-necked shirt and as he lay with closed eyes the scar was only a mark on his face. Watching him she thought his cheeks seemed fuller and his skin less sallow than on their first meeting.

Sensing her gaze he opened his eyes and pushed himself up on one elbow. "What are you thinking?"

"Nothing in particular," she smiled. "Except perhaps how different it is here in the spring than in the winter."

Down the garden a squirrel had appeared on the fence. The dog, lying alongside Michael gave a yelp of indignation, and raced hell-for-leather towards it. The squirrel leapt for the trunk of a birch that overhung the garden, clung there for a moment, then flew upwards as if jerked by elastic. It reappeared a few seconds later at the end of a branch, rubbing its forefeet together impudently while below the dog barked its frustration.

"He hates them," Michael told her as they both laughed. "He spends the whole summer chasing them out of the garden."

Sarah patted the indignant dog as Michael called it back to them. "Poor old Robbie. You mustn't let them upset you like that or you'll get ulcers."

As silence returned, bringing with it

the distant hum of cars, she remembered the task she had set herself. "We really ought to take advantage of these long evenings. Why don't we run down to the coast sometime? And perhaps call in a pub for a drink on the way back."

There was an immediate change in him. "What's the matter? Are you getting bored coming here?"

"Of course I'm not bored. But it would be a change to go out one evening, wouldn't it?"

"Aren't you getting a change soon? Isn't your husband taking you to Italy in August?"

"I wasn't thinking of myself — I was thinking it would be a change for you."

He was now staring moodily at a magpie preening its wings in the near-by apple tree. "I don't like pub-crawling. And I hate beaches crowded with trippers."

"That's hardly what I had in mind. I was thinking of going somewhere like Chapmans Pool. And calling in some quiet country inn on the way back isn't my idea of pub-crawling."

His bitterness was now of pre-Christmas vintage. "What do I buy you a drink with?

Sea shells from the beach?"

It was a point she had not considered and her reply came spontaneously. "All right — let's make a bargain. You take me to the coast and to a pub for a drink the next time you sell a story. How does that sound?"

Was she procrastinating again? Weeks and months might pass before he made a sale. Yet the very uncertainty of it was in her favour as his sarcastic reply indicated. "You mean to say you're prepared to wait as long as that? All right, but don't blame me if your tongue's hanging out before we make it."

She laughed. "It won't be that long. You're certain to sell that last short story once you find the right editor."

With his trust in her almost complete she was now receiving the full flood of his ideas and their originality and diversity astonished her. In the beginning, blaming his isolation, she tended to think them naïve and unrealistic: then she began wondering if he did not possess a unique gift for seeing the simple truth when others, better educated, wove for themselves webs of self-deception. Once she had seen herself as the guide whose task was to lead him back into society. Now she began to realize that the very stimulation of his ideas, in spite of their rancour, was beneficial and that this bitter, twisted man might have as profound an effect on her life as she hoped to have on his.

Of the many ideas that intrigued her, three were incorporated in short stories about marriage, written, as he told her, 'for himself'. The first one concerned an eighteen-year-old girl whose personal security had been undermined by quarrelling, incompatible parents. Escaping to London she found the cold indifference of the metropolis equally unbearable and when a young man proposed marriage she saw it as a deliverance from her loneliness. Yet it was not long, after having a child, that she realized she had escaped only into a trap. Her husband was unimaginative and unambitious, his friends no better, and the narrowness of her existence began to chafe her more and more. When, inevitably, her resentment turned on her husband and their quarrels began to bring misery to the child, it became clear the wheel had turned its full, ironic circle.

"If you're saying that people shouldn't marry only to escape their circumstances, then I agree with you," she said, after reading the story.

He shook his head impatiently. "It's not just the circumstances they run from. Most people are scared of loneliness, some of personal responsibility, some of their own identities. Isn't marriage an escape from all these things?"

It was an aspect she had not considered before. "I suppose it is, to some people. But if it helps them escape, isn't that a good thing?"

"Not in the long run. If you don't develop your own personality, if you rely on someone else to prop you up all the time, you not only remain half a person, you also become a damned bitchy one because you live in constant fear of someone stealing your support."

"And you think it's that kind of insecurity that makes people quarrelsome and jealous?"

He nodded. "I believe it's one reason. Everyone has a fundamental need to

120

develop their own personalities. If you deny it, either to yourself, or to your partner, you end up by scratching one another's eyes out. You must have seen it dozens of times. Frustrated middle-aged couples giving one another hell and not knowing why."

She had never been more attentive. "But this isn't the fault of marriage; it's the fault of people who use it either for escapism or domination. Surely it provides as good an opportunity to encourage one's development as it does to restrict it."

He gave her a reluctant grin. "No-one's denying that. But how many see it that way."

His second story was about a highly intelligent young man who married a beautiful but less complicated girl. With the girl full of admirable virtues, the man remained in love with her but could not surrender his need for friends of his own intellectual level. As some of these friends were girls, his wife, already feeling insecure because of her intellectual shortcomings, began to accuse him of having illicit love affairs. Eventually, although the story made it clear they were both still in love, the marriage broke up.

It was a tragic little story that brought an immediate protest from her. "This is saying love can't succeed between two people of different intellectual levels. I can't accept that at all."

Although he still found it difficult to accept criticism, the fact she now dared to make it was a measure of her progress. "If you read the story properly, it says nothing of the sort. You don't need to be intellectual to stimulate a person. All I'm saying is that the more complicated a person is, the more friends or acquaintances he'll need. If you like, we're like radios: the more complicated we are the wider our waveband of frequencies. No-one can hope to stimulate them all — that's impossible when each one of us is unique. What usually happens is that we fall in love with someone whose compatibility enables them to reach a wider waveband than most."

She was quick to see the implications of his argument. "This is also saying that the more complicated the man, the more likely he is to get into tangles with women. Once in a while he meets someone who stimulates an unfulfilled waveband and, boom, he's in love. Isn't that right?"

He shrugged. "Of course. Isn't that how it happens? Only don't make the mistake of thinking that one person takes the place of another."

"What's that supposed to mean? That we can love two people at the same time?"

He looked surprised. "Of course. Why not?"

"If by love you mean what I mean, then I can't agree with you. I couldn't love two men like that. And neither could ninety-per-cent of the women I know."

His sudden hostility startled her. "And what do you mean by love? Sex?"

"That's a part of it, yes."

"A part of it! Be honest, for God's sake, and admit you can't see the difference. Being in love . . . making love . . . they've brain-washed us about it for so many hundreds of years we've even ended up with only the one word. So is there any wonder we're as miserly with one as we're possessive about the other?"

Uncertain of his meaning, she would have liked to question him further but his hostility forced her to humour him.

"You're talking like the Flower People now. Isn't that their philosophy — that one should love all and sundry?"

His bitter reply, biting deep into the core of her own marital grievances, made her suddenly aware what she was hearing. "And you're talking like all those other smug bastards out there. Don't throw any love about — the world's got too much already. Keep it all for yourself and your own little brood. Christ, what a great job the Church did for love and the brotherhood of man when it invented the holy sacrament of marriage."

His bitterness towards the Church for its concept of love showed in his third short story. This was about an earnest young clergyman whose sermons to his congregation were full of praise for the benefits of matrimony. His stepbrother, an atheist and a divorcee, derided his views and told him there was no surer way to physical and moral enslavement.

In time a young girl of the parish took the clergyman at his word, turning her charms on him to such good effect that in six months the two were married. Previously the young vicar had spent most of his spare time visiting the sick and the lonely; now he found himself expected to devote more and more time to his demanding young wife. The birth of one child and then a second tightened the chains even further until at last, to his dismay, he was left with time only for the rituals of his office and none for its humanities. The story ended with the stepbrother saying that as the Church had made the strait-jacket it was perhaps only justice its ministers should wear it.

"I'm not certain I understand this," she told Michael after reading the story. "Are you blaming Christianity for the war between the sexes?"

"Did I say Christianity? I thought I said the Church."

"All right, the Church. What's the difference in this context?"

"Oh, come off it. I'm no Bible puncher but I know the original Gospels hardly mentioned sex relationships. It was misogynists like St Paul who did the damage. Women were a bit unclean — hadn't they betrayed Adam — and sex could only be tolerated if it was made into a religious affair and called a congress of love. And it was a human catastrophe."

"A catastrophe!"

"Yes. Because if love meant anything at all it meant charity and forgiveness; a man wanting his wife to be happy no matter what it cost him. Sex, on the other hand, had taken such a beating from the Church that it had been turned into a punitive thing, making a man feel that if his wife had a wandering eye God was with him if he punished her. When the two were lumped together and institutionalized, you ended up with people actually proud of their bloodymindedness because they believed it proved the depth of their love."

She understood something of what he meant. "It's always puzzled me how a person can claim to love someone one minute and be wanting to scratch their eyes out the next."

"Right. By pretending love and sex

are the same thing those old priests gave everyone a perfect opportunity to be bastards and gain sympathy at the same time."

"Yet some Institution like marriage had to be evolved, if only for the protection of children."

"Maybe, but they didn't need to make it the prison it is. Can't you see, that by thundering hellfire and damnation to the adulterer for hundreds of years, the Church made every man and woman a prison warden of his partner? And so made real love in marriage damn nearly impossible."

She hesitated. "But aren't people slowly coming round to the idea that love and sex are somehow different things?"

His hard stare challenged her. "Are they? Sometimes I think the opposite. At one time a couple of young men could be good friends, share a flat, go out together, and none thought anything of it. Now it's ten to one they'll be thought homosexuals."

"Surely it's only people like television playwrights who paint that picture. And isn't that only because it's become fashionable and profitable to write about homosexuals and lesbians?"

"I'm not saying there isn't a cult and a clique cashing in on it. Even the Edwardian deceit that everyone was pure and shining wasn't as absurd an exaggeration. But I still think it's the belief that love, affection, or whatever name you care to use, must always express itself in sex because one is a part of the other that makes the cult possible. And it's a tragedy in itself because a whole area of human companionship is being tainted these days and perhaps lost because of it."

It was an angle she had not considered before and she listened in fascination as he went on: "But come back to marriage again and the demands it makes: 'Till death do us part' — no matter how vile or disgusting a man's habits become, the poor devil he marries has to put up with them until one of them dies. What sort of incentive is that to make a man behave like a civilized human being? And the one about your partner having a right to your body. A man comes home stinking drunk and unless you sleep with him you're breaking your marriage vows. That's so disgusting it had to be thought up by a misogynist. One has a privilege to a person's body. Never a right."

Her laugh was one of respect. "Just the same, I think you're a bit hard in blaming the Church for sexual jealousy."

"Why? I'm not saying there might not be other causes too, but in the Western world it was the Church that thundered hellfire from every pulpit and made us all throw stones at one another. So why shouldn't it take the blame?"

"I wasn't meaning that. To me, sexual jealousy is a part of human nature."

His lips curled in contempt. "Here we go. Good old human nature. The age-old excuse for behaving like a bastard."

"But it isn't only Christians who're jealous, Michael. You get it everywhere. You always have."

He shook his head. "Wrong. You get it only when people have a religion that's obsessed with sex. What about the Greeks in the days of Pericles — said to be one of the happiest times in history. What about the Polynesians and the Eskimos? If sexual jealousy was basic, they'd have suffered it too. Few if any 'instincts' are basic. Modern psychology says that — not me. It's age-old conditioning that makes us respond like ape-men with clubs."

"But if you're right we could get rid of it."

"So we could. But who wants to — we like our jealousies and our bitchiness. To get rid of them we'd need a new society with an entirely new set of values."

Thoughtful now, it was a moment before she spoke. "I don't know I agree about jealousy but I can see your point about sex and love. In a way you're saying one is the enemy of the other."

"They are when sex is possessive, as in our culture. As I say, we can't do much about that as yet — we're a hundred years from even deserving a better way of life. But at least we could teach ourselves and our kids to recognize one emotion from the other. Otherwise we'll go on kidding ourselves it's our 'Great Love' at work every time we tear an old sweetheart to pieces."

His attack on the Church was still worrying her. "If you're right, why do all of us behave in the same way? Seventy per cent of us never go near a church these days unless we're going to a wedding or a funeral."

He showed impatience again. "I've just explained — behaviour patterns come from tradition, laws, literature — the whole ethos of a culture. As ours are based on the Jewish and then the Christian beliefs, atheists and agnostics act and think like everyone else."

Ideas, ideas, ideas — some amusing her, some depressing her, some startling her. But of all she heard from him, none was to have such an effect on her in the days ahead as those three bitter, short stories.

9

THE last week in June she arrived at the cottage to find a subtle change in him and she wondered if he had suffered a relapse. Patting the fussing dog in the passage for a moment, she glanced up at him.

"Have you any news for me?" It had become a stock weekly question: the disappointments of a young writer seemed endless. This time, however, he did not answer immediately and her voice quickened.

"What is it? Have you had some good news at last?"

It was obvious the bitter creature within him was trying to diminish his pleasure. "I've sold that last short story, if that's what you mean. I got the letter this morning."

Excitement brought her upright. "Oh, Michael, that's splendid news. I'm so glad. What's the magazine called?"

"*Woman's Star.* Don't you remember,

the editor scribbled on a rejection slip a few weeks back that she'd like to see more of my work."

There had been so many false alarms and dashed hopes that she had feared his stamina would not hold out much longer. But this sale would give him a new lease of life.

"It's quite a good magazine, isn't it?"

"Not too bad. They're going to pay me twenty guineas."

It seemed little enough for his months of work but she was careful to give no hint of it. "This is just the beginning — from now on you'll sell more and more. What did the editor say in her letter?"

"You can read it if you like. She wants me to try a three-part serial for her."

She read the letter and laughed her delight. "This is wonderful. They're sure to pay more for serials. Aren't you excited?"

He shrugged. "I've got to think of an idea first. Then it has to be written and then she has to accept it. So where's the point in getting excited?"

"It's good for you to get excited. What you've done once you can do again.

Come on, Michael — smile. Your luck's started to change. I think it calls for a celebration."

His start reminded her of the promise she had forced from him. Nervous of the outing herself, she pushed aside the temptation to ignore it. Opportunities of this nature came rarely enough. "Instead of eating here, why not go to the coast and have a picnic?" she asked. "It's a fine evening. And on the way back we'll call at a pub and have a drink or two."

He turned away. "Not tonight. I don't feel like it."

"Why not? It isn't six yet — there's plenty of sunshine left."

"I can get all the sunshine I want in the garden. But if you feel like going, no-one's stopping you."

She braced herself. "What about that promise you made me? I've been looking forward to this evening for a long time."

He muttered something, then met her eyes again as he saw a way of escape. "How the hell can I take you? Getting an acceptance doesn't mean I've got the money — that might not come for another month. So what do we celebrate with?"

She took a pound note from her handbag and handed it to him. "That's all we shall need — less, in fact — and you can pay it back to me when the cheque comes. Come on, Michael," she urged as she saw his trapped expression. "I'm only asking you to come for a drive to the coast and to have a drink with me on the way back. You surely can't refuse me a small favour like that?"

It had been her intention to drive through Worth Matravers to St Albans Head but as they left the village he motioned to a gravel lane on their left.

"If you want a really quiet place, that's the road to take," he muttered. "When I first came down here and had a shilling or two to spend on petrol, I sometimes came here with Robbie. You can walk for miles without seeing a soul."

Although it was against her purpose to take him to a place as deserted as this, she decided it was perhaps wiser to win his confidence in easy stages. "All right. It sounds just the place for a picnic."

She felt a slackening of tension in herself as she turned down the lane:

traffic had been heavy between Wareham and Corfe Castle. The gravel track led them round a hill shoulder and ended as a disused quarry. As Michael opened the car door Robbie leapt out with a joyous bark, raising the heads of sheep grazing on the adjoining hill-side. Michael followed, carrying a shopping bag she had packed with sandwiches and coffee.

There was a slight breeze but it had little edge to it. As they started for the cliffs Sarah realized it was the first time she had walked more than a few paces alongside him. His limp did not slow their progress, nor did it hinder him in negotiating the two stiles that lay between them and the cliffs.

They walked westwards along the cliffs for fifteen minutes and chose a spot to picnic between two headlands. The view was superb, the massive chalk cliffs marching towards the distant smudge of Portland Bill. With larks singing overhead, they ate the sandwiches and drank the coffee. No-one came down the cliff path and the headlands remained deserted as she offered him a cigarette.

"You certainly found yourself a peaceful

spot. Did you come here often?"

"Quite a bit, that first summer," he admitted. "But I haven't been more than a couple of times since."

Was that only because he had no money? Or was it, as she suspected, that a withdrawal from life such as he had made fed upon itself and made every attempt to escape that much more difficult?

She lay back, listening to the silence. Although the headland to their right was now in shadow, the sunlight was still golden in the valley. The silence had a creamy quality, moving languidly to the rhythm of the waves. Iridescent colours glowed in her half-closed eyelashes: she felt completely relaxed and astonishingly content.

"You haven't said anything about your novel for a long time," she said. "Are you still working on it?"

"Yes. On and off."

"How far have you got with it?"

"I'm on the second draft. About a third of the way through."

She gave a laugh of surprise and rose on her elbows. "You mean to say you've already written one version and haven't told me?"

As he nodded and turned away she noticed the buttons of her green nylon shirt had pulled open, exposing her low-cut brassière. His eyes had been resting there: almost his first acknowledgment in eight months that he saw her as a young and attractive woman. Her hand was rising to fasten the buttons when she paused. He would be able to see her from the corner of his eye and if she were so quick to make the adjustment he might, in his hypersensitive way, take it as a rebuke. She lay back again instead.

"You've done all that work on top of the short stories you've been writing. When have you found the time?"

He shrugged. "I've worked on it in the evenings. It was something to do during the winter."

She wondered how long his health would last at this rate. "You've kept this a secret from me, haven't you? I don't even know what the theme is."

"I thought I'd like you to read it as a new r)vel. It would help you to criticize it better."

That pleased her. "When can I have it?"

"It'll be some time yet. It's not an easy book to write."

At that moment Robbie's bark made both of them turn their heads. On the headland above, a middle-aged man and two young girls had appeared and were descending the path towards them. With Michael's eyes remaining on them she took the opportunity to button up her shirt.

She drove back through Kingston and paused on the hilltop to show him the view. To the south the evening sky was luminous with a single, bright star. The two hill ridges were soaked in twilight and between them the ruins of Corfe Castle rose in their haunting sorrow. Corfe Castle had always affected her that way, like a piece of music whose message one could not quite gather but whose sadness caught at the breath. She glanced at Michael.

"To me this is the loveliest view in England. I could sit for hours looking at it."

He nodded, his eyes turning back to the

139

view. This was something you couldn't do with John, she thought, at least not with an easy mind. Sooner or later he would come out with: 'Hadn't we better be moving, darling — it's getting rather late?' so that you knew immediately he had been enduring it for your sake. Poor John — her thought was enveloped in affection — the material world would never allow him to escape. You could feel it — pulling, pushing, filling his mind with statistics so that beauty never had more than a precarious tenancy.

She drove down into the valley. Night had already settled there: she had to use her headlights in the twisting lanes. Beside her she could feel tension growing in the silent man. Lights appeared ahead and as they drew nearer she saw they belonged to a small country pub. As she turned into the car park and switched off the engine he turned aggressively towards her.

"What's the idea?"

She feigned surprise. "I thought we'd agreed to have a drink on the way back."

"You wanted it, not me. I hate pub-crawling."

"But we've something to celebrate. Please, Michael, we won't stay long."

"I don't want a drink. No-one's stopping you — go and have half-a-dozen if you feel like it. But leave me alone. I'll wait here with Robbie."

"What about your promise?" she asked quietly.

In an instant he was the self-destructive man she had met the previous year. "For Christ's sake, what are you — some sort of dipsomaniac? Can't you spend just one night a week without a glass in your hand?"

She couldn't complain, she thought. She had taken the task on with her eyes open. "Don't cover up by insulting me. You made me a promise. Are you going to keep it or not?"

She heard his heavy breathing, then he suddenly cursed and jumped out of the car. The slam of the door as he flung it closed made the dog bark in alarm. Closing her own door she ran after him and caught up with him in the porchway. As a car drove down the lane, illuminating them both for a moment, she saw the scar was a huge, disfiguring brand that changed his entire expression. Afraid what it might signify, she lost courage and caught hold of his arm.

"It doesn't matter. Let's go back to the cottage."

He cursed again and threw off her hand. "No. You want your damned promise keeping, so let's do just that."

Without another word he pushed the door open and walked inside.

10

THE room was warm and smoky, with glinting brass and the loud hum of conversation. Three men propping up the counter turned to stare at them as she caught hold of Michael's arm again.

"Michael, please. Not now. I'd sooner go back to the cottage."

He jerked away. There was a trace of sweat on his forehead and the scar made his expression almost unrecognizable. "What do you mean — not now? You've got what you wanted, haven't you?"

"I know but I've changed my mind. We can come some other time."

"To hell with that. We're here — let's get it over. What do you want to drink?"

She was agonizingly aware that his behaviour was attracting the attention he would ascribe to his appearance. The three men were still watching them curiously and at a table near the end of the bar a teenage girl had nudged the young man alongside her and was whispering to him. The man, ruddy-faced and over-dressed, looked as if he might be a local farm worker. Others were turning their heads and the hum of conversation was fading. Not daring to argue any longer she pushed him towards an empty table.

"Come and sit down. I'll get the drinks — I need some cigarettes."

To her relief he made no protest and she approached the bar. A man reached it ahead of her and she was forced to wait while he was served. Behind her Michael had pulled a piece of paper from his pocket and was pretending to study it, but his stiff posture, sweating face, and above all the triumphant scar, betrayed his state of mind. As she waited the palms of her hands grew sticky from tension.

The three men at the bar had resumed their conversation but the teenage girl's curiosity was as avid as ever. Watching her, Sarah felt a hot prickling of hate. Couldn't the cruel little bitch see what she was doing to him?

She took him back a large brandy. As she offered him a cigarette she noticed the violent trembling of his hands and had a rush of panic. I've pushed him too far, she thought. What in God's name do I do now?

Drinking her martini as quickly as she dared, she smiled at him. "I enjoyed that. Now I suppose we'd better start back. If we hurry I'll have time for a cup of coffee."

Across the table his suffused eyes were hostile. "I've still got a pound to spend — remember?"

"I don't want any more to drink, Michael. Not tonight. Keep it for another time."

His chair scraped back. "We're spending it tonight. Sit there and wait for me."

At first she had thought his refusal to leave was punishment for the ordeal she had inflicted on him. Now, as she watched him limp towards the bar with his eyes moving belligerently from face to face, she realized his mood was more complex and more dangerous. The self-destructive elements in him had been aroused and wanted an excuse to fight. If she could not get him away before he had much more to drink the consequences might be serious.

The teenage girl was whispering to her young man again as he neared their table. Aware from Michael's every movement that he was conscious of her interest, Sarah half-rose from her chair. To her relief, however, the young man seemed embarrassed by the girl's curiosity and did not turn his head.

Michael returned without incident to the table. She made a massive effort to lighten his mood but the scar appeared to have gained complete control over his personality and she could draw nothing from him but sullen monosyllables.

He finished his second brandy quickly and rose again. This time she caught his hand. "No more, please. Two's all I ever have. Let's start back now — I mustn't be too late tonight."

His hostility seemed to burn her. "This was your idea, not mine. Go if you want to but I'm having another drink."

Behind him another couple had entered the room and were joining the teenage girl at her table. As Michael started towards the bar the girl leaned forward to whisper to them. Both turned. The second girl had a pretty, vacuous face; the youth a sallow, somewhat pimply complexion. As Michael neared them she said something that made the youth laugh. Whether it concerned Michael or not, it was the match that set fire to the fuse. Changing direction Michael went right up to the youth. Sarah could not hear what he said but the mixture of alarm and belligerency on the youth's face told its own story. As she jumped to her feet the second girl's voice shrilled out.

"What's it got to do wi' you what he was laughin' at? Why don't you mind your own business?"

The rest came in a series of disjointed impressions. She heard Michael curse and saw his fist rise and strike the pimply youth's jaw. Then she found herself pulling him across the room, to be pushed violently away as they reached the doorway.

"Michael," she choked. "For God's sake come away. Michael, do you hear me?"

Panting, he stood there as if his one wish was to fight every man in the room. "Damn them," he snarled. "Damn the smug bastards to hell."

All conversation had ceased and for a

moment the scene was like a tableau. Across the room, with the two indignant girls alongside him, the pimply youth was holding his jaw. Through the hanging cigarette smoke, astonished faces were gaping at them. Gritting her teeth, she caught hold of Michael again.

"Come on. Pull yourself together. We must get away."

Another blurred moment followed and then she was alongside the car and struggling to push him inside. "For heaven's sake hurry. They might call the police."

Terrified someone would run outside to take the car number she accelerated wildly down the road. Michael, now looking fully aware of what he had done, seemed frozen beside her. As her breath returned and her heart stopped hammering, she turned to him. "I think it's all right The youth wasn't badly hurt and I don't think anyone took the car number."

He could not hide his relief although he said nothing and gazed back at the road. Feeling it better to leave him to himself, she drove the few miles to the cottage in silence. As she pulled up on the grass verge and glanced at her watch, his sullen voice broke the silence.

"Well, are you coming in for coffee? Or are you too fed up with me?"

All the way from the pub she had been trying to decide the right things to say to him. "It was a stupid thing to do, Michael. It might have got you into serious trouble."

His eyes avoided her. "All right, don't give me a lecture. I know it was stupid but I couldn't help it."

She knew the time for evasion was over. "Why not? What was it that provoked you?"

His protest was violent. "Oh, come off it, for Christ's sake. You know that as well as I do."

"All right, we won't pretend any longer. You've got a scar down one cheek and on account of it you hate mixing with people. Have you ever stopped to think it could be an excuse instead of a reason?"

The white blur of his face turned towards her. "What the hell does that mean?"

"When Judy left you, you turned bitter and declared war on the world. But you had to give yourself a reason for opting out, so you blamed your disfigurement, the reason Judy left you. You convinced yourself it had turned you into a kind of freak and since then it's been the shield you've been hiding behind."

There was a short, dumb-founded silence. Then his jeering laugh leaped at her. "What do you think you are — a trick-cyclist or something?"

"It's not that difficult to work out — I'm surprised an intelligent person like you hasn't done it himself. When you're in the cottage you're as good-looking as any other man, better than most. But as soon as you meet a stranger, get upset, or start talking about the past, the scar distorts your expression. It's your mind that brings about the change, not the scar, but it provides an ideal excuse to live like a hermit and avoid people."

"Why the hell should I want to do that?"

"I think it's because you've been badly hurt once and subconsciously don't want it to happen again," she said quietly.

His laugh mocked her again. "I mustn't

miss this. You're saying my face screws up in case someone thumps it? Right?"

She nodded. "I couldn't have explained it better. The point is, it wouldn't happen at all if you lost your dislike of people."

"And how the hell does one do that?"

"I suppose you start off by trying to trust them more. Or perhaps by finding compassion for them in the way you find compassion for them in your stories."

He looked astonished. "Compassion — in my stories?"

"Of course. Every story's full of it. That's the thing I find so strange about you. You can forgive people in your work but not in your personal life. Perhaps that's because, like me, you're more afraid of them than anything else."

For a moment the intensity of his stare was almost frightening. Then, as if giving himself time to absorb what he had heard, he patted the restless dog before turning back to her.

"This is why you wanted me to go out with you tonight, isn't it?"

"Of course. I felt that if we could meet a few people together you might start to get your confidence back."

"And instead I took a smack at one of them."

"Yes. But I hope you realize it wasn't him you were hitting."

"You mean it was Judy?"

"Wasn't it?"

He turned away without answering. Through the open window she could smell the heath and the warm, pregnant earth. In the silence an owl hooted and before its eerie cry had died away the light breeze ran down the hedge alongside them in a patter of leaves. An idea suddenly came to her.

"Tell me something. Would you say I was a normally attractive woman?"

His start betrayed him. "You! Of course I would. Why?"

"Nothing, except my opinion of a man ought to carry a little weight. And I'm telling you there's nothing whatever wrong with your looks. That scar can even look attractive — when you're not carrying that chip on your shoulder. Lose that and you can face anybody with confidence."

"So it's only a chip I'm carrying now?"

She smiled at him. "It's a fairly big

152

chip — I'll admit that — but with an effort it's nothing you can't get rid of. Supposing you do me a favour and try?"

He gazed at her, then gave a twisted grin. "What about coming inside for a cup of coffee?"

She knew she ought to be home by this time but with the tide running in her favour she felt unable to refuse. "All right, but it'll have to be a quick one."

Neither of them spoke about the events of the evening or their conversation in the car until she was leaving. He saw her to the front gate and paused there. "I'm sorry about tonight. I was a damn fool — it might have got you into trouble."

"That's all right," she said. "We probably won't hear any more about it."

She sensed there was something else he wanted to say as he frowned and gazed down the dark lane. The sky was luminous but the heath had a blackness that seemed to accentuate the loneliness of the cottage. After a few seconds he turned back to her. "If you still want me to go out with you after what happened tonight, I suppose I could try to be a bit more civilized."

He waited at the gate as she drove off. With her mind full of the evening's happenings she had reached Poole crossroads before she realized it was well past midnight.

11

SHE knew there was trouble facing her the moment she turned into the drive. The evening television programme had long ended but a light was still burning in the sitting room. She drove into the garage and switched off the engine and the headlights. Their glow remained on the retinas of her eyes for a moment before she was plunged into darkness. As she edged by the car and fumbled for the garage switch, the side door of the house opened and yellow light spilled out on the drive.

John was standing on the step, wearing slippers and a dressing gown. She pulled down the garage door and started towards him. Her shoes made a brittle, uncertain sound on the gravel.

"Hello, darling. Sorry I'm so late but I couldn't help it tonight."

He moved aside for her to enter and closed the door. "I've been worried about you," he muttered. "Do you realize it's nearly one o'clock?"

The thought that she could be wrong and his vigil was due only to concern made her contrite. "I'm very sorry, darling. You shouldn't have stayed up — I'd have phoned if anything was wrong."

As her eyes became accustomed to the light and she saw his expression her apprehension returned. Some of his emotions she could identify: there was embarrassment — whenever John was embarrassed he could never look one straight in the eye. There was resentment, the sulky look of a little boy who feels he is not getting all the attention he deserves. These normal symptoms of his possessiveness did not worry her: she was concerned with the unidentified emotion behind them. Was it mere uneasiness? Or could it be actual suspicion?

She took off her coat and threw it over a hall chair. "You shouldn't have waited up," she said again. "I'll always phone if I'm in any trouble."

"Where from?" he muttered. "Eunice's?"

He's phoned me there, she thought, and now he's trying to trick me. For the moment shock blinded her to the unfairness of her resentment. Before she had time to answer he glanced back at her, either ashamed of his suspicions or afraid to have them confirmed.

"Mother rang earlier this evening to ask if we'd mind going round on Friday instead of Thursday and I phoned you at Eunice's to check you weren't doing anything. I thought she sounded rather embarrassed and . . . "

"And when you questioned her, she told you I'd left," she interrupted. "Is that it?"

She thought relief appeared in his eyes. "Yes. What puzzled me was that she didn't know where you'd gone. So when you weren't home by midnight I naturally began to get worried."

Her own emotions were mixed now. She knew part of his desire to believe her came from genuine affection and this made her ashamed of her falsehoods. At the same time she found it not altogether displeasing that a draught was blowing at last into his self-satisfied world.

"It's all simple enough to explain," she said, making him follow her into the sitting room. "The other week I ran into an old school teacher of mine who came down to Bournemouth to retire. She's had a bad stroke that's paralyzed one side of her face and it's made her so sensitive she hardly ever goes out these days. Feeling sorry for her I promised to go round one evening and when Eunice had a friend visit her after dinner tonight, I thought this was a good opportunity. One thing led to another, we'd a lot to talk about, and I stayed later than I intended. And that's all there is to explain."

What a glib liar you and Michael are turning me into, she thought, sharing her resentment in equal parts at that moment.

Her explanation had given John time to conquer his relief and to find another complaint. "But why didn't you phone me? Surely you must have realized I'd be worried."

She damned him for another lie. "The old lady hasn't a phone — she can't afford one on her pension. And you can't very well go wandering around the streets at that time of night looking for a kiosk."

His mood was beginning to change.

"You say this old woman was one of your school teachers?"

"Yes. Miss Phillips. A sweet old thing."

"Why didn't you ask her round here one evening?"

"I did, but I could tell she didn't want to come. The whole side of her face is paralysed and she's terribly sensitive about it — neurotic, in fact."

"Where does she live?"

"In Parkstone. Not far from the road out to Bere Regis."

"Has she a car?"

"No. I told you — she's quite hard up."

He was silent for a moment, then gave a shrug of resignation. "In that case I suppose we'd better call on her sometime, hadn't we, and take her out for a drive? We might even do it next week — we have a couple of free evenings."

To have aroused his sympathy with her lies seemed intolerable. "I'm afraid she would be just as sensitive about that as coming here to meet you."

"But surely I wouldn't make her uncomfortable?"

The sudden brittleness of her voice

alarmed her. "Leave things as they are for the moment, John. Take my word she wouldn't enjoy it."

"All right. I was only trying to help."

Shame took her to his side. "I really am sorry to have worried you. I ought to have phoned — I see that now."

He gave an embarrassed laugh. "You know how it is — you start thinking about road accidents and that kind of thing."

"I know." Reaching up, she kissed him. "I'm truly sorry, darling."

"The trouble was, I couldn't imagine where you could have gone at that time of night. Apart from Mother, the only people I could think of were Harriet and Robert."

She stiffened and drew sharply back. "You didn't phone them?"

"Yes, as a matter of fact I did."

She turned away. "Whom did you speak to — Harriet?"

"Yes. She was worried too — it was after eleven when I phoned. She rang back half-an-hour ago to see if you were all right — I thought it very decent of her."

Panic was fluttering inside her like a tiny, trapped bird. Harriet, agog at the news, trying to learn more under the pretext of friendly solicitude. She turned back to him with a smile.

"Then you'd better phone back and tell her I'm home, hadn't you?"

His eyes moved to the electric clock on the mantelpiece. "Won't they both be in bed by this time?"

It was not possible to hide all her bitterness. "Not Harriet. If you don't ring her, she'll ring you."

He gave her a puzzled look as he moved towards the door. As she followed him the phone began ringing. She shook her head as John paused and glanced back at her.

"No, you talk to her. Tell her I'm safely back and that I'll give her a full account of my movements when we all meet next week."

Before he could answer she ran past him and up the stairs, not quite certain what she was escaping from.

Her first thoughts the following morning were that it was too risky to visit Michael for a week or two. Although she believed she had quelled John's suspicions, Harriet might easily revive them when they all met the following Monday, and there was always the chance he might phone Eunice again to reassure himself. She could, of course, warn him beforehand that she intended to visit the fictitious old lady again, but John belonged to a club near Parkstone and if he suggested meeting her afterwards a whole set of new problems might arise.

Deciding to spend a Wednesday evening or two with Eunice until the silt settled, she sat down to write Michael a letter but soon her pen slowed and stopped. He would receive the letter on Friday: it would condemn him to at least twelve nights with only Robbie and the radio for company. God knows, four hours a week of human companionship was little enough: it still left a hundred-and-sixty-four hours of loneliness. The brutality of the statistics made her eyes close. What did John or Harriet know about that kind of loneliness? She doubted if either of them had been utterly alone, without a friend for miles, for a single night of their lives. She certainly had not.

Once more her mind beat at the restrictions that shackled her. The most she was allowed to be was a one-armed Samaritan: because Michael happened to be a man her help became an illicit thing. No-one had warned her before marriage that it entailed a sacrifice of freedom as profound as this: no-one had warned her that one day it might force her to choose between her conscience and her vows.

But what vows denied her this human right? To love and honour? Did one love less by feeling concern for the welfare of others? Did one honour less by honouring the urges of one's conscience? It was easy to feel bitterness towards John, and bitterness she felt at that moment, but she also knew that while others might condemn him, few would behave differently in his place. With the possessive concepts of marriage long sanctified, it was all too easy to find shelter behind them.

She decided she could not inflict the disappointment on Michael by letter. With little of importance to do that day she would drive out and explain in person. About to run upstairs to change she remembered Eunice. Ideas were coming fast now. She would phone her and change the time of her arrival the following Wednesday. In this way she could spend the afternoon with Michael, as in the past, and be with Eunice in the evening if John were to phone.

She thought Eunice sounded a little breathless. "Oh, hello, Sarah. I've been hoping you'd phone. Was everything all right last night?"

Sarah found the girl's anxiety oddly irritating. "Yes. Why not?"

"I'm so glad. John sounded so surprised when I told him you weren't here. Did you tell him about the old lady?"

"Yes. I hadn't much choice."

"I didn't know what to do at first. Then I remembered you asked me to say I didn't know where you'd gone. It worried me afterwards because I felt he might think it strange you hadn't given me a reason for leaving early."

And you think there's something a little strange too, don't you, Sarah thought. Even although you're Eunice and absolutely loyal. She brought her resentment to heel. It hardly became her to resent a little curiosity — not when Eunice had lied for her and at her own request.

"It was stupid of me to ask that because it didn't matter. Only I do want to keep him away from her."

"Did he ask to see her?

"He suggested we invited her round here one evening or took her out for a drive and I tried to explain why we couldn't."

"Did he understand?"

"Yes, I think so."

"Good." Eunice sounded as if she had lost a burden. "So in the future it doesn't matter if he knows where you've gone?"

"Not really. Except — " she wondered how she could put it to prevent Eunice growing curious again " — if John knows I go there often, he'll feel more and more obliged to take a hand and it'll be difficult to go on refusing him. So I think it might be a good idea for a few weeks if I see her on Wednesday afternoons and visit you afterwards — in other words switch the times around. You wouldn't mind that, would you?"

Eunice sounded enthusiastic. "I'd love

it. It's the evenings that drag so much. And it means you'll be here in case John phones again. What about dinner — will you have it with her or with me?"

"We don't need to make a hard-and-fast rule there, do we? She might want me to stay for dinner now and then but I can always let you know beforehand."

She allowed Eunice to chatter on for a few minutes more and then went upstairs to change. As she closed the side door fifteen minutes later and was walking towards the garage she heard the muffled sound of the telephone ringing.

The significance of her quickened pulse as she turned back was not lost on her: her need for secrecy was not only affecting her nerves, it was giving her a sense of guilt. Half expecting it to be John on the phone, she gave a start at the purring voice that greeted her.

"Hello, darling. Are you alone or is John still there?"

"Oh, hello, Harriet. No, he's gone to work. Why?"

"I'm just being tactful, that's all, darling. Whatever happened last night?"

"Didn't John tell you?"

166

"He said you'd been visiting an old friend. But earlier in the evening the poor poppet sounded terribly worried. I told him he was being silly but when he didn't ring back, even I began to wonder if something had happened to you."

The last thing she wanted at that moment was to antagonize Harriet but it was not easy to hide her resentment. "From all the fuss everyone's making one would think I'd stayed out all night."

Harriet sounded amused. "You know me. I'd say the best of luck to you if he had what it takes."

Like hell you would, the girl thought. "I'm afraid it wasn't that exciting. Just a lonely old lady who'd asked me to visit her."

"How disappointing, darling. I thought for the moment you might have met one of those foreign students that Bournemouth's full of these days. One of them made a pass at me the other day and you can't believe how tempted I was."

Two minutes later Sarah went out to her car again. John, Eunice, and now Harriet: all of them, whether aware of it or not, with a seed of doubt planted in their minds. From now on every move she made would have to be planned and executed with scrupulous care. It was a prospect that chilled her in spite of the warmth of the day.

12

SHE arrived at the cottage just after eleven-thirty. Unused to seeing her on consecutive days, Michael showed some apprehension as he opened the door.

"Hello," he muttered. "What's brought you out today?"

"It's a fine morning and as I've something to ask you I thought I'd take a run out."

"Something to ask me?"

She walked past him into the living room. The kitchen door was open and seeing a wash pail standing in the sink she turned to him with a laugh. "What's this? Wash day?"

"Yes, I put a few things in to soak earlier on." He was watching her closely. "What happened? They didn't get your car number, did they?"

"No, it's nothing like that. I came to ask if you'd mind my visiting you in the afternoons for a few weeks instead of the evenings."

"Why? Because you were late home last night?"

She decided it was better to tell the truth. "Yes. John was waiting up for me. It's not serious," she said quickly as he turned away. "But I'll have to be a little careful for a few weeks."

The question he had long avoided came out at last. "Then he doesn't know anything about me?"

"No."

"Why not?"

She gave a half-laugh. "I could hardly tell him if I wanted to go on seeing you, could I? Not without bringing him with me."

"You mean he'd believe we were having an affair together?"

"Wouldn't any man?"

There was a silence, then his sudden, jeering laugh. "He's one of those we've talked about, isn't he? Tells you he loves you in one breath and checks your car mileage the next. What did he do last night — give you a beating for not being in by curfew?"

Attacks on John were the one thing she could not take from him. "Don't talk like that please. You don't know anything about him."

"Don't I? You've given him away a hundred times in the things you've said. He's a 'together man', isn't he? Smile together, wash the babies together, spend your money together. The advertisers love him — they catch him on TV every night. Don't be shy — go together when you buy. Christ, I don't know how you put up with it."

His perception added to her anger. "Stop exaggerating. A man liking his wife at his side doesn't necessarily mean he's possessive."

"Demanding she's at his side does! Refusing her any liberty of choice does. Treating her like a possession does. Why haven't you the guts and the honesty to admit it?"

Her control snapped. "Stop being so damned black and white about everything. Just because your wife was jealous and a bitch as well doesn't mean that everyone else who's a bit possessive is the same. I admit John's got this one fault but there's nothing wrong with the rest of his nature."

"In fact the sun shines out of his wallet, doesn't it?" he sneered. "Why not admit that as well?"

She took a deep, steadying breath. "Please don't attack John any more, Michael. If you do, I'll have to go."

Cursing, he limped towards the door. "What's stopping you? Get back to your loving prison warden. And stay there in the future or he might put extra guards on you."

It was the triumphant scar that checked her. "I don't know why we're quarrelling like this. I'm still going to see you each week, the same as before."

She had to offer him a cigarette before he would unbend. "What exactly happened last night?" he muttered.

To minimize his hostility towards John she watered down the incident. "John's been under the impression I've been visiting a girl friend on Wednesday evenings. Last night he phoned there and she had to cover for me. I managed to smooth it over but you must see I'd better be at Eunice's for a week or two until he's forgotten about it."

"You mean in case he checks up on you again?"

When she did not answer him he turned away bitterly. "If things are as bad as that you'd better pack the whole thing in. I don't want you to lose your comfortable meal ticket for me."

"You're exaggerating again," she said sharply. "If the worst happened I could explain everything to John and it would be all right. But I don't want all that fuss when there's no need for it. Not when I've only to change the times I see you."

He dropped into an armchair and lit the cigarette. Bitterness hung over him like a cloud. "Why bother?" he muttered. "In any case someone's going to press a button one of these days and the whole bloody lot's going up sky high."

She tried to laugh. "They've been saying that for a good number of years now but we're all still here."

His bleak eyes lifted in dislike. "More's the bloody pity. Cheating, grabbing, bitching — as far as I'm concerned the sooner it's over the better."

She did not know which she feared

most — his shafts of hurt malice or his moods of dejection. Although she stayed with him until three o'clock she could not cheer him up and she drove back both depressed and apprehensive.

The following week, as she feared, Harriet was not slow in bringing up the happenings of Wednesday night. With her silken legs folded beneath her in the armchair, she looked as pretty and innocent as a kitten as she glanced across at Sarah.

"Darling, do tell us more about this old lady you've been visiting — she sounds so pathetic. Did she really teach you at school?"

"Yes. She was my history teacher."

Harriet made a moue of distaste. "All those horrible dates and things — I hated history. Does she come from the Midlands too?"

"Yes. At least I think so."

Harriet looked reflective. "I wonder what made her come to Bournemouth. I mean, you'd think an old person like that would retire to the place where she had friends and relatives, wouldn't you?

Particularly after having this stroke."

"It happened after she came to Bournemouth," Sarah said, damning her. "Sometime last year."

"Poor old thing. A disfigurement like that must be an awful thing for a woman."

As Sarah nodded she noticed Robert was shifting about uncomfortably in his armchair. Before Harriet could continue he leaned forward. "You must both be looking forward to your holiday. When do you leave?"

"Two weeks on Sunday," Sarah told him, grateful of the diversion.

Harriet gave an envious sigh. "Three weeks in Italy — and all Robert's giving me is a fortnight in Cornwall. But the old lady's going to miss you, isn't she?"

Sarah gave a start. "Miss me? Why should she?"

Harriet's violet eyes opened innocently. "I thought you'd been seeing a good deal of her recently."

Seeing John had turned to listen, Sarah felt the hard rapping of her heart. "What ever gave you that idea?"

"I suppose I took it for granted you'd been doing what you did last week — going round to see her after visiting Eunice."

"How could I do that? I only ran into her a few weeks ago."

"Oh, I see. I hadn't realized that, darling. I thought you'd been visiting her for some time."

Women like Harriet could not survive without making mischievous conversation, Sarah told herself in bed that night, and suspicion did not necessarily lie behind it. But each time she was close to reassuring herself, the memory of Robert's embarrassment would return and keep sleep from her.

In an effort to compensate Michael for the cancelled evening visits, Sarah made two extra trips out to the cottage during the next fortnight, and on two occasions took him out to his favourite place on the Dorset cliffs. Going out in the afternoons with him when, in theory at least, her friends were at work or at home, took some of the strain from the excursions and when, on the second outing, she persuaded him to go into a restaurant with her for lunch — an occasion that proved uneventful — she felt entitled to believe that in one area at least she was making progress with him. It was this encouragement that made his behaviour on the Friday before her holidays the more disappointing.

She had already visited him on Monday that week and, with the idea of shortening the long gap to her next visit, she had arranged to see Eunice on Friday instead of Wednesday. A steady rain was falling from a grey sky as she drove down the lane to the cottage. It was a visit she had been dreading and the sight of Michael at the door confirmed her worst fears. Some weeks ago he had allowed her to buy him a new pair of slacks and a pullover on condition she took the money back when he received payment for the short story. These clothes he usually wore when she visited him. Today, although aware she was coming, he was back in his tattered pullover: a deliberate gesture, she felt, and one that filled her with apprehension. Wanting to keep his mind off their separation as long as possible, she began talking about his work almost as soon as she entered the cottage.

"You didn't say anything about the three-part serial when I came on Monday. How is it coming along?"

The cottage was chilly and he had knelt down to light the paraffin heater. He answered without turning his head. "It isn't. I've been working on the novel this week — I want to get it finished."

Concerned, she drew closer to him. "Is that wise? Isn't it better to get the serial finished while the editor's interested?"

He lit the wick and closed up the heater without answering.

"Michael, I know what this novel means to you, but you do need money rather badly, don't you? I thought we'd both agreed this was the chance you'd been working for."

At that he swung aggressively round. "Chance? The chance I want is to attack the hundred-and-one things in this world that I hate. Not to sit on my backside writing fairy stories."

"I know that. But I don't see what else you can do at the moment."

"Of course you don't see," he gibed. "You're one of *them*, aren't you? You'll talk about principles, but when it comes to the crunch you'd sell every principle you ever had to keep your fur coats and your Continental holidays."

The brief glimpse into the cause of his mood made her wince. "Whatever your principles, you still have to pay your bills. I'm not asking you to give up your novel — I'm asking you to wait a week or two until the serial's finished. I know it's difficult when you have so many ideas, but put first things first."

"And first things are money, aren't they?" he sneered.

"In this case I suppose they are. But don't blame me because the world finds money so important."

"Don't blame me! Don't blame anybody! Just keep on accepting that money maketh the man. You'll be telling me next it's human nature that makes us this way."

"Isn't it?"

"My God!" His contempt was like a lash. "Can't you understand we're like this only because we get the same conditioning that Genghis Khan gave his Mongol hordes? Swoop in and grab all you can lay hands on. Never mind who or what you destroy in the process — grab!

And then defend what you've got to the death. Isn't that the message we get from the first slap on the bottom to the last nail in the coffin?"

"You're exaggerating and you know it."

"Exaggerating, hell! We've gone further. We don't just make the non-grabbers feel failures — we round 'em up and exploit them as well. I suppose you'd call that progress."

She made the mistake of trying to argue with him. "You're surely not saying Man hasn't become more socially conscious over the last two hundred years."

"We've made no progress worth a damn," he snarled. "What about the Nazis and their concentration camps? What about Joe Stalin? What about Hungary, Sharpeville, the Congo, Biafra, Czechoslovakia? What about the thousand million people out there at this moment whose kids go hungry every day? What about the bastard scientists who find in every new discovery a better way of killing people? There hasn't been a real philosophical breakthrough since Jesus Christ on the Mount and they've done a great job fouling up that message. We've got planes instead of donkey carts, we've got H-bombs instead of stone axes, but my Christ we're the same barbarians using them."

She withdrew cautiously. "I can see what you mean but it hasn't much to do with your finishing the serial, has it?"

"You can't see anything. Why should you want new ideas? Human nature's done all right for you — your cave's stuffed with loot. So why sell it out by admitting it could be changed?"

"I'm not asking you not to express your ideas," she said quietly. "I know you'll never believe me but there are some I like very much. But you have to live while you write, and this serial gives you the chance. So write it and keep faith in the meantime."

His lips curled. "You can sound an awful prig at times. Keep faith in what? Land of Hope and Glory?"

"Faith that one day your ideas will be published."

"In this country? When even talented novelists can't pay the rent because the bloody public libraries give their work away free? If they can't survive, who do you think's going to publish me?"

"I still believe people with original ideas can make themselves heard if they try hard enough."

In moods like this his masochism would allow him no comfort. "Who wants to make himself heard, anyway? Who cares what happens to this rotten cesspool of a world? Everyone thinking about himself and covering it up under a smokescreen of concern for others — to hell with it all."

She knew he wanted a quarrel with her: it was the way he fought his pain. She moved towards the kitchen. "I feel like coffee. Do you mind if I make some?"

He shrugged sullenly. "What right have I to mind? Didn't you bring me a tin of the stuff last week?"

He remained moody and quarrelsome until after lunch when for a brief while she succeeded in lightening his mood. Worried about his financial position she brought up the subject of the serial again and this time won a grudging promise he would complete it before resuming work on the novel.

His first direct mention of her holiday came half-an-hour before she was due to leave for Bere Regis. Robbie, unable to go outside because of the rain, had been scuffling restlessly around the room and Michael had called him over and was patting him. As the dog, enjoying the attention, rolled over on his back, Michael glanced up at her.

"So on Sunday you're off with your husband to the blue Mediterranean?"

It came out so casually that for a moment she believed he had succeeded in accepting the parting philosophically. "I'm afraid so." Then, unwisely. "But three weeks will soon pass."

Contempt was a sudden flame in his eyes. "What do you mean — you're afraid so? No-one's taking you at the point of a gun, are they?"

"Michael, we've gone over all this before. Your own common sense must tell you I can't get out of it."

"And of course you want to, don't you? Three weeks will soon pass." His sarcasm and mimicry were cruel. "Three weeks does soon pass, when you're having a good time. But try three weeks in here with only the radio to listen to and then see how quickly it passes." The dog ran under the desk as he leapt to his feet. "But what the hell do you care — you won't give it a second thought once you're back home among your friends."

It was the beginning of the worst ordeal she had been called to face in the cottage. The scar, his evil genius, spared her nothing. "I've got you sorted out. You're the kind that enjoy scattering bits of sunshine around as long as it doesn't cost you anything. But have to give up something you enjoy, like three weeks in Italy, and it's a different story. People like you are worse than the others — you pretend to give but actually you give nothing. And for my money that's the worst kind of hypocrite."

His torrent of invective confirmed her fears. Once she had left him feeling her visit had been of benefit. Now, while he was far happier to see her, his mood changed for the worse on her departure and she drove home apprehensive for his well-being. She had tried to ridicule this apprehension but listening to him now she felt it was justified.

She could do nothing with him until the torrent of accusations began to run dry. "Whatever you say or believe, I still wish I wasn't going away on Sunday," she said, "but that gets us nowhere. Will you promise to take care of yourself and to write me at least twice a week?"

He had moved to the desk to hide his shame. "What do you want that for? I won't have any news."

"I'm not worried about news. I just want to hear from you."

"How can I write you without your husband finding out about me?"

She laid a piece of paper in front of him. "I've written out a poste restante address for you. Send your letters there and I'll pick them up." When he did not answer she went on: "Until now I haven't asked many favours of you, Michael. But this is important to me, so promise you'll do it."

He gave his harsh laugh. "What's worrying you? Do you think I'm going to put my head in the gas oven as soon as you've gone? I'd have thought that would be a relief. No more insults and no more lies to tell your husband."

"Please. Will you write to me?"

"Yes, all right," he muttered. "Only don't expect many letters. I hate writing the damn things."

He accompanied her to the front door. Rain was still falling from the grey skies, dripping from the cottage eaves and making familiar pools on the path. Meeting his bitter eyes, she reached up and kissed his cheek before running out to her car.

Twigs from the hedge brushed against her window as she drove out, a last appeal for her to stay. Before accelerating down the lane she paused a moment and glanced back. It was a mistake: his expression was something she was not able to forget in the days ahead.

Eunice's telephone rang just before eight o'clock that evening. "It's that friend of yours, Harriet," the girl said as she returned to the sitting room. "She's phoning from Bournemouth."

Sarah's anger was tempered by dismay as she picked up the receiver. "Hello,

Harriet. What do you want?"

"Hello, darling. I hope you don't mind my phoning you at your friend's."

"Why should I mind? But how did you know I was here tonight?"

"Because I've got ears, darling. You told John you were changing your evening this week when you were at our house on Tuesday. I had to phone you tonight because of a mix-up we've had over Palace Court tickets. I bought two for tomorrow night when I was in town this morning. only to find Robert had collected two more at lunch time. As we're rather stuck with them we wondered if you and John would care to come along. They won't be together, of course, but we could meet afterwards and have a farewell drink."

"Couldn't you have phoned me early tomorrow morning? Then I could have asked John."

"Not really. Robert's seeing a couple of friends later this evening and he thought he'd pass them on if you didn't want to go."

"Then that's what you'd better do. I don't want to go out tomorrow — I haven't finished packing yet."

"I was afraid of that but was hoping for the best. All right, darling: I'll tell Robert to get rid of them." Harriet sounded more like a purring cat than ever as she went on: "How is the old lady, Miss Phillips? Have you seen her this week?"

"No, I haven't."

"Poor old thing. I felt so sorry for her after you'd told me what had happened. I suppose you wouldn't like me to run round and see her one evening while you're away? I'd be only too glad to help out."

"You know that's impossible. I told you why."

"You did, dear, but do you think old people like that always know what's best for them? I mean, the more she cuts herself off from people the worse she might get. Don't you think so?"

Sarah knew her face was pale. "It's not what I think, Harriet — it's what she wants. I'll have to ring off now — Eunice is expecting a long-distance call from her husband."

"All right, darling. I'll give you another

ring before you leave on Sunday. Bye now."

The girl found she was trembling as she lowered the receiver. You bitch, she thought. You suspicious, crafty bitch.

13

SARAH found her first few days on Elba had an almost convalescent agreeableness. With her mind still in England, she found the hot sun, the mauve mountains, and the turquoise sea induced a dreamlike condition in which she could think about Michael without the moral responsibility of taking action. She was safe from Harriet, safe from John, and yet could not accuse herself of fecklessness.

She received her first letter from Michael six days after her arrival, collecting it from the General Post Office in Portoferráio while John was taking a lesson in skin diving. It was a short note that said little except that he was working on the serial and he hoped she was enjoying herself. Curt, almost unfriendly as it was, the very knowledge he was well sufficed her at that moment.

It was during the second week, when her lagging mind caught up with her body, that her inner conflict began. Suddenly the mountains sprang into focus, the warm sea began stroking her body sensually, the blue grapes broke sweetly on her tongue. Now it was the lonely heath, the crackle of frost, and the huddled cottage that seemed of another world, and she began to feel the stir of disturbing questions. A quarrelsome, neurotic man with the ambition of becoming a writer — could she not have sentimentalized his problems? Instead of encouragement, would it not have been wiser, morally and practically, to have given him the advice John would have given — get a down-to-earth job and stop living in the clouds? Her doubts alarmed her in many ways. At one moment she wondered if her distance from the lonely Dorset heath was giving her an objective clarity of vision she had lacked before: in the next she wondered if she was a fickle, inconsistent woman swayed first into excessive sentimentality and now as easily turned into a sybarite by the hot Tuscan sun.

These anxieties induced in her a curious ambivalence towards the island. She would dislike it and then, an hour later, be enjoying its pleasures even more than John. He had hired a car on their arrival and they spent much of their time touring, pausing when the mood took them to explore a village or to take a swim in the warm sea. She was quite happy with him again: on holiday and with no excuses to display possessiveness towards her he could be excellent company. Also the island seemed to relieve him of his inhibitions: his love-making was not only more amorous but also more spontaneous. In turn it made her feel closer to him and that she might have exaggerated the problems of their relationship.

One day towards the end of the second week they explored the lovely old mountain town of Marciana. In the piazza — an old-world place of cobblestones, oleanders, and a running fountain — they listened for a while to an itinerant band of musicians playing Neapolitan airs. Afterwards they wandered up worn steps higher into the town. The light was vivid, white sunlight and velvet shade. Donkeys, with huge wicker panniers hanging from their saddles, passed them in the incredibly narrow alleys. Linnets chirruped at them from white-washed walls. Bougainvillaea swept them like cool red flames as they walked past. Everything now was colour: the mazarine sky, the datura, the crimson oleanders. Even the silence, Sarah thought, that the sleepy doves made palpable, was like magenta velvet.

The alleys grew steeper and more deserted. They climbed a series of steps and paused for breath on the edge of a tiny, cobbled square. She caught John's arm in delight. "Oh look, isn't that beautiful?"

Cottages stood on each of the three sides of the square, a tiny church on the fourth. Huge stone pots of flowers stood outside the cottages, their blooms vivid splashes of colour against the sun-bleached walls. The church had a square, white-washed tower with a gilded clock. The slightest movement of the hot air brought the incense of heliotrope and jasmine.

They stepped forward into the hot, dazzling sunlight. Sarah would have liked to go inside the church but the door was locked. John was standing in a corner of the square and she walked across to him. He was gazing through a gap between the cottages and she saw that the mountain dropped sharply for a few hundred feet before swelling out into terraced vineyards. Opposite them was another mountain range and to their right the great sweep of the Tyrrhenian sea.

The hot sun burned her shoulders. The incense of the heliotrope came again and suddenly she felt as if something long-starved had opened up inside her and the hot colours and the scents were pouring in. She had known nothing like it since her youth when at orchestral concerts her very being had seemed to melt and be absorbed in music.

She stood in ecstasy and surrendered herself. The mazarine sky seemed to pour down, the lucent sea to rise towards her, the air, alive with a million specks of golden dust, to sink through her skin. The sunlight splintered on her eyelashes and thrust a hundred iridescent spears into the willing womb of her mind. She drank and drank and felt she could never be satisfied.

It was John turning his eyes to the cottage on their left, who broke the spell. Although its flowers were tended, the vacant appearance of the windows showed it was unoccupied. "How would you like a view like that from your bedroom window every morning?"

She nodded eagerly. "It's beautiful, isn't it?"

"I wonder if the speculators have got in yet. If they haven't, I'll bet you could clear your capital on a place like that in a couple of years. It's a long tourist season on this coast."

Drugged with beauty as she was, she could hardly believe her ears. His tanned face, smiling regretfully, turned towards her. "It's all wishful thinking, of course. There'd be too many snags over currency transfers. But wouldn't it be marvellous to own a dozen or so cottages over here?"

It was a moment made more cruel by the compatibility they had seemed to share during the last two weeks. Afraid of its significance she found herself making excuses for him. Real estate was his career and careers meant more to men than to women. But when the excuses were made and accepted, an indefinable sadness remained.

Altogether she had three letters from Michael. They were all brief and said little — he was not a good letter writer. She wrote him more often — not an easy thing to do when she and John were together most of the time and shared only one hotel room. It meant equally brief letters — sometimes only postcards — and she dared not imagine what Michael made of their brevity.

A further problem was Michael's sensitivity. Not daring to talk about the island or what she and John were doing, she was driven into talking about him, and with his news so scarce each of her letters tended to become a painful repetition of its predecessor, in the main reminding him to take care of himself until her return.

She had one letter from Harriet, a letter as calculatingly affuse as its writer. 'We hope you are having a wonderful time, darling, and are getting gloriously tanned. How many of those marvellous, crisp Italian males have made a pass at you — dozens, I'll bet — you lucky thing.' Everything very friendly and as sincere as the lick of a cat, but Sarah sent a card back. She knew it was appeasement but she was afraid of Harriet now.

On the plane back to England her feelings were hopelessly confused. During the holiday she had been closer to John than for many months and the last thing she wanted was the gap to widen again once they were back home. Added to this was a dread of the scenes Michael so often forced on her. On the island life had been wonderfully straightforward and uncomplicated. Now the tightrope walk was to begin again: the lies, the deceptions, the dangers. Instead of refreshing her strength for the ordeals ahead, the island seemed to have sapped it and made her long for the simple and veridicous life.

Yet beneath it all, half-buried by this time, she was conscious of the stirring of memories, and as she dug down to them her mental image of Michael began to take new shape. During the last two weeks of her holiday she had tended to remember the more unprepossessing aspects of his character and had wondered if it had been a form of self-protection, an inverted seduction that made easier her desire to live in contentment with John. Now she found herself remembering once more the causes of Michael's intractability and her sense of responsibility came back. With his trust in humanity shattered through no fault of his own, had she not made herself indispensable to him by asking for his trust? Would not his relapse be worse — perhaps even disastrous — if she abandoned him now? She could not tell him for her own security: her conscience would exact too high a price.

There was no escape: she had to resume her visits no matter what the consequence. But on that flight home she was like a soldier returning from leave, cherishing the last hours of safety before being plunged into danger again.

14

SARAH and John arrived back from Elba on Saturday and on Sunday paid a duty visit to John's mother. Sarah found something almost symbolic in the masculine forthrightness of Mrs Ashley (with its unapproachability) after the voluptuous yet winning wiles of the island. The conversation on the happenings in Bournemouth while they had been away, on golf, on the weather, on real estate, all seemed to merge into three words that rang dully inside her. They were back, they were back, they were back.

She visited Michael the following morning, leaving the house less than half-an-hour after John left for the office. She could not analyse her emotions as she approached the cottage but she was nervous. Red berries showed on the wild hedge as she backed her car through the gate and a few rust-speckled apples hung on the aged trees. There was a late summer dryness in the leaves of the hydrangea that brushed her dress as she edged by the car and approached the door.

As she reached it she heard Robbie's sharp bark. Almost instantly there was a stumble of footsteps in the passage and Michael wrenched the door open. His eagerness seemed to take both of them by surprise and brought a lump into her throat.

"Hello, Michael. May I come in?"

His defensive mask fell into place. "Hello," he muttered. "I didn't expect you until Wednesday. When did you get back?"

"Saturday evening." His appearance dismayed her. The slight tan he had acquired before she left on holiday had gone and his cheeks and body were as gaunt as on their first meeting. He was wearing his old slacks and his open-necked shirt was frayed and soiled round the collar.

"You've lost weight," she accused, as she followed him into the living room. "You haven't kept your promise and been eating properly."

He offered her a cigarette. "I've had

enough. Would you like some tea?"

"In a moment. First sit down and tell me everything that's happened while I've been away."

"Everything that's happened?" His stare was hostile. "What do you think I've been doing — throwing wild parties? You're the one who's been living it up, not me."

She had known the pent-up bitterness of three weeks must come out sooner or later. "I know how lonely you must have been."

"You don't know anything," he said harshly. "I don't think I've been to the door half-a-dozen times and then only to pay the baker and the grocer. The rest of the time I've been working and wondering what the hell I live for."

She gave a start. "What do you mean by that?"

He dropped sullenly into a chair. "Nothing. Forget it."

She knew it was the last thing she would be able to do. "I wish you wouldn't talk like that. Tell me what you've been working on."

"I've finished the serial, if that's what you're getting at."

"Oh, good. When?"

"I posted it off ten days ago."

There was a furtiveness about him now that quickened her interest. "Have you heard anything yet?"

He inhaled on his cigarette. "It's been accepted. I heard last Friday. They're going to pay me ninety pounds for it."

She started, then gave a laugh of delight. "Michael, that's wonderful news: I couldn't have heard anything better. Now you've got something to subsidize your novel. Aren't you thrilled?"

He shrugged despondently. "Things don't give you the same kick when you're on your own. In any case, when you've had the number of rejections I've had, how the hell can you feel excited about anything?"

It was a remark that reminded her of the need to get him out of the cottage. "I still think it calls for a celebration. Change your clothes and let's go out for a few hours. We'll have lunch in a pub somewhere."

His reaction told her he had been expecting the suggestion. "For Christ's sake, you haven't been in the place five minutes and you want to be off again. I know it must seem a dump beside the places you've just been to, but you don't have to make it so damned obvious."

She pushed aside the temptation to give in to him. "It's only a minute since you complained you haven't been out of the cottage for three weeks. The change will do you good. We can go to a quiet place for lunch."

"Where do you find quiet places at this time of the year?"

"We'll drive right into the country. Into Dorset. Please, Michael. I want you to get some fresh air."

He hesitated, then cursed and turned away. "You're no sooner back than you're pushing me around. Why the hell can't you take me as I am?"

He came downstairs five minutes later wearing new slacks and a clean shirt. "Come on if we're going," he muttered. "I don't want to be late back — I've some letters to write today."

The irony did not escape her as they drove off. Neither of them wanting the outing and yet forcing themselves to go for the sake of the other. At first the traffic was dense and her nervousness returned until she reminded herself it was not Wednesday and she had told John no lies about her movements. If she were seen, she could always say she had gone for a drive and given a young man a lift.

She drove as far as Cloud Hill and paused on the summit. "This is another view I love. Have you been here before?"

As he shook his head she saw again his ability to be absorbed in scenery. She drove on towards Sherbourne and seeing a small roadside pub with a thatched roof she swung into the car park. "It's nearly one o'clock. Let's have a beer and something to eat."

He followed her inside with no more than a frown of protest. The three elderly men leaning against the bar did not give them a second glance. Insisting that Michael went to a table, she brought beer and rolls over to him. As a young woman and two more men entered the bar and he showed only minimal embarrassment she felt both surprise and relief: her few outings with him appeared to be having their effect at last.

Heartened by the thought she had a sense of well-being that was in complete contrast to her earlier mood. As he returned from the bar with topped-up glasses of beer she reached out and squeezed his arm. "I'm enjoying this. Aren't you glad now that we came out?"

He was still not able to show pleasure. "It is a change, I suppose."

"Of course it is. You need to get out more. Once you get the money for the serial you'll be able to use your motor cycle again, won't you?"

"If it doesn't cost too much to put it back on the road. I haven't used it since early last year."

"Has this editor said she'd like more serials from you?"

"She says she'd like another short story. I haven't done it yet, though — I've been finishing the novel."

"Finishing it? You were only halfway through the second draft when I went away."

"Don't forget I've had three weeks to work on it. You can do a lot twelve hours a day, seven days a week."

She ignored the jab. "You've been

working too hard — that's why you've lost so much weight. Have you got a manuscript I can read?"

"I've a carbon, yes. Although it might be pretty messy — I didn't have time to correct both copies."

"Does that mean you've already sent the original off?"

He nodded. "Last Saturday. To Martin and Cranston."

She could not hide a start of surprise. "They're very good publishers, aren't they?"

"What does that mean?" he asked sardonically. "You think I've been too ambitious?"

She did her best to deny it. "Don't be silly. If you have faith in it, why shouldn't you send it to a good publisher?"

With her personal anxieties dulled by his good news she suggested they drove back through Lulworth and Kimmeridge. "I haven't been round that way for ages, and it was a favourite run of mine when we first moved down to Bournemouth."

He shrugged. "I don't mind if you've got the time."

"I don't need to start back until four

o'clock. And it's such a beautiful day."

The traffic became heavier the moment they reached the Dorchester Road but she had the feeling nothing injurious could happen to her today. She drove through Kimmeridge to Swanage and then took the road over the Purbecks to Corfe Castle. On the way she found an unoccupied lay-by and drove into it.

"This is another of my favourite views. I always think Poole Harbour looks wonderful from up here."

Below, the great, cloud-shadowed heath ran down to Shell Bay and to the vast mirror of the harbour with its green islands. Beyond it Bournemouth was a white blur on the rust-hazed horizon. She stayed there until they had smoked a cigarette, then turned the car towards the road where she had to pause as a long stream of traffic went past. As one car, an Austin Cambridge, drew level, she thought the driver, a woman, turned to stare at her. The impression was fleeting, there was a sharp bend ahead and the car was out of sight within seconds, but it was sufficient to change her mood and remind her of the risks she was taking.

Back in the cottage he handed her his novel, a bulky manuscript in a makeshift folder. "This looks exciting," she said. "I shall start reading it tomorrow. Then we'll be able to talk about it when I come on Wednesday."

"You are coming on Wednesday just the same?"

"Yes, of course. About two o'clock, if all goes well."

He saw her out to the car where she laid the manuscript on the seat beside her. Seeing him watching her, she gave the folder an affectionate pat. "You can't imagine how much I'm looking forward to reading this."

His smile was wry. "Let's hope you're not too disappointed."

"I won't be," she said confidently, closing the car door and smiling at him through the open window. "But we'll talk about it on Wednesday. Take care of yourself until then."

He followed the car to the gate where he spoke without glancing down at her. "Thanks for coming to see me today. I hadn't expected you so soon."

Her surprise puzzled her as she drove

208

away until she realized it was the first time she had heard him thank her for anything.

The next morning, when her chores were finished, she fetched the novel from her car and took it into the sitting room. As she sat a moment gazing at the bulky manuscript on her knee, success took on a new meaning for her. It was a relative thing, the distance a man travelled in spite of his handicaps, and with these so often subjective, difficult to assess even for those who cared. But there were times, as now, when one knew something of the adversities faced and overcome, and as the girl held the novel in her hands she felt a fierce, almost maternal pride.

The story concerned a young, immigrant Jamaican who arrived at an isolated Northumbrian village to find work. Unused to colour and suspicious of the Jamaican's ingenuous nature, the clannish North-countrymen closed their ranks and drove him from job after job. When he became friendly with a local girl, her rejected boy friend and work-mates laid wait for him and beat him up. Jobless and embittered, he became easy prey for a criminal gang who needed an expendable decoy to cover their movements. Abandoned by the gang and captured by local villagers who now had a righteous outlet for their hostility, the Jamaican turned on them and killed a man, for which he received a life sentence. The village, with its invaders repelled, settled down once more to its coursing and pigeon racing. All was well in the Realm again.

It was four o'clock before Sarah turned over the last page and she was a long time setting her thoughts and emotions in order. The background, she felt, was completely authentic and the Jamaican was also a success — in parts his suffering and, inevitably, his loneliness were harrowingly portrayed. In addition, as in most of Michael's short stories, there was a certain power — she had always wanted to go on reading.

On the debit side she felt there were too many minor characters and they fell well short of the Jamaican — perhaps because Michael's personal bitterness had influenced him into making them more symbols of prejudice than real people.

There was only one sympathetic character among them, a married woman of the Jamaican's own age, and in the end even she surrendered to her husband's intolerance and abandoned him.

Biased as she was towards the novel, she found it difficult to assess its chances of publication. Yet her overall reaction was one of excitement and she retained this excitement on her arrival at the cottage on Wednesday.

To her surprise she found Michael's welcome casual to the point of indifference and it was only when she noticed how his eyes avoided the manuscript beneath her arm that she understood. She waited until they were in the sitting room, then turned to him.

"I've read your book and I think it's splendid. In fact I enjoyed it so much I read it all in one sitting. So you've got your first fan."

He gave a deprecative laugh as he took the manuscript from her. "I didn't expect you not to like it. Not you."

"What does that mean — that you didn't think I'd give you an honest answer?"

"Not necessarily. But I've always known it would have to be pretty bad for you to say so."

It was an opportunity for straight talk and she took it. "If I'd said it was no good, you'd have believed me immediately. You've no confidence in yourself and you hate the world so much you're never happy unless it's taking a kick at you. Sorry I can't oblige. I like the novel and if that doesn't please you I can't help it."

From the way he stiffened she was prepared for a quarrel. Instead he moved a few steps towards the window, then suddenly turned to face her. "You wouldn't fool me, would you? You are on the level?"

Unprepared for this, she had a sudden lump in her throat. "I'm on the level, Michael. I like your novel. Now let's sit down and talk about it."

He dropped into a chair and pulled out his cigarettes. As she saw the trembling of his hands it was suddenly there — the loneliness and vulnerability of the creative writer. Months, perhaps years, of dedicated work, building an elaborate structure whose every brick was a new act of imagination. Alone, unaided, with no guarantee that the whole edifice was not based on a subjective misconception. Until the moment came, as now, when the first reader was faced and a thousand hours of travail awaited judgment. It was a responsibility that suddenly intimidated her.

He talked to her about the story deep into the afternoon and from his questions she knew his trust in her was now complete. With her gratification was a growing fear that in her enthusiasm she might have exaggerated the chances of the book's success.

"Michael, if the manuscript should come back from Martin and Cranston, promise me you won't be too disappointed."

His mood changed instantly. "You don't think it's good enough for them, do you?"

"I never said that. It's just that you've sent it to the foremost publisher in the country, and you've said yourself how hard it is to get a first novel published. So if it comes back, don't get depressed, just send it to another publisher instead.

Will you promise to do that?"

He shifted restlessly in his chair. "There isn't much else I could do, is there?"

"Yes. You could take it too much to heart. And with dozens of other publishers to try that would be stupid."

Her warning seemed to quell his enthusiasm and he hardly mentioned the book again that afternoon. Before she left, however, she succeeded in lightening his mood again and as she opened her car door he checked her.

"You couldn't possibly come in the evening next Wednesday, could you? Only next week. I know you can't do it often."

"Why next week?" she asked curiously. "Is it your birthday?"

To her surprise, he nodded. "Yes, but that's not my real reason. The money for the serial ought to be here by then and I thought I'd like to take you for a drink somewhere. But don't come if it's going to cause any trouble."

She was finding it difficult to accept the significance of his offer and to realize how close to victory she was. "If it's your birthday, of course I'll come. I'll be here for dinner — that'll leave us the whole evening free. Where were you thinking of going?"

He was already looking embarrassed by his gesture. "I don't know — you know the places better than I do. Think about it and we'll decide when you come next week."

15

ON Friday that same week John took her to a dance at his golf club, an informal, end-of-the-summer affair held in one of the club's own rooms. A four-piece band provided the music, candles on the tables lent the room intimacy, and after three dry martinis Sarah began to enjoy herself. The sense of well-being gained from the holiday was still with her, and with John more attentive than he had been for years and with Michael apparently on the road to recovery, the problems that had loomed so large a week ago now seemed dramatically shrunken. After a fourth martini her optimism could not be contained. At any time Michael would break out of his self-imposed exile and her responsibility towards him would lessen. John, in his turn, would lose his possessiveness and the claustrophobia of their marriage would give way to a generous, more trusting relationship.

She was sitting at a table with Robert, watching a Paul Jones. John was dancing with a small blonde girl and Sarah thought how handsome his Italian tan made him appear. A sudden desire for him both amused and delighted her. You're such a fool, John, she thought. Why can't you realize how much I could love you if you'd only give me the freedom to love?

The music changed tempo and the dancers changed their partners. Sarah's eyes moved to Harriet who was now dancing with an elderly man of distinguished appearance. It was fascinating to watch Harriet dance, the way she simulated interest in the man and the way her petite, mini-skirted body leaned back in his arms. How much of it was instinctive — the predatory female — and how much was calculated Sarah had never been able to decide. Tonight however she was prepared to give Harriet a large slice of the doubt.

She glanced across the table at Robert. Robert had always given her the impression of being shy when left alone with her. At the same time she sensed his relief at being freed for a few minutes from

Harriet's gynocracy.

Feeling he might misinterpret her glance as a reproach for not inviting her to dance she turned back to the floor. The couples were parting again in a swirl of colour and mini-skirts. John had been left by the music in front of Harriet and another girl, and was in the awkward position of having to make a choice. As he hesitated, Harriet, free of such inhibitions, ran forward and threw her arms around him, forcing him to hold her tightly. Flushing and laughing she danced away with him, her blonde hair very close to his cheek.

Robert's awkward shuffle in his chair told Sarah he had seen the incident. "You don't mind sitting this one out, do you, Sarah? I've never been one for Paul Jones."

"I was hoping you wouldn't ask," she smiled. "I always get some goon who stands on my feet."

His good-natured face grinned in relief. "Good. Let's have another drink while we're waiting."

She was certain he had spoken to take her mind off the incident. Poor Robert, she thought. What secret miseries did Harriet inflict on him over the years?

John had the next dance with her. "Enjoying yourself?" he asked, his lips nuzzling her hair.

"Yes. It's rather fun, isn't it?"

"It's the holiday," he told her. "It's helped you to relax again."

She nipped at birth the resentment that he should attribute all the blame to her. "Perhaps it has. I certainly enjoyed it."

"So did I, darling. Let's go there again next year."

Back at the table Harriet had a complaint against Robert's elder brother, Arthur. "We never hear a damn thing from him or his wife during the winter and yet every summer he scrounges a free holiday from us. They arrive on Monday, complete with their long-haired, sulky kid."

"How long are they coming for?" Sarah asked.

"Only a week, darling. We can't afford them any longer. They like pub-crawling too much and as they haven't a car we're dragged out almost every night with them. Why don't you ask John if he'll come along with us one evening? Then we'll be able to talk about something else but kids and television."

John had been talking for the last few minutes with two of his golfing acquaintances, Bob and Ann Gregson, who had stopped beside their table. As Sarah turned towards John she saw all three of them were gazing at her. John's hardened expression, his 'possessive' look as she secretly named it, told her instantly something was wrong.

She felt her smile turn stiff. "I'm sorry. Were you talking to me?"

Ann Gregson, a fluffy blonde, answered her. "I was just asking John what you and he were doing out our way on Monday. We live in Studland these days and I thought I passed you coming out from a lay-by on the Corfe Castle road. You do have a green Renault, don't you?"

Sarah felt hot needles of panic digging into her forehead. Beside her Harriet's eyes were suddenly intent, and she knew that unless she responded quickly suspicion would fall on her no matter what she said. She took a deep breath and nodded.

"That's right. I was out that way on Monday. The house seemed a bit close after our holidays and I went for a drive. On the way back I passed a young serviceman thumbing a lift and took him as far as Poole. That's who you must have mistaken for John."

Ann Gregson's laugh sounded embarrassed. "I thought it was you. How did you enjoy Elba? John said you had glorious weather."

"We did. I enjoyed it very much."

They had no sooner moved away than John turned on her. "You never told me you went out on Monday."

Her throat was dry. "I never thought to. Nothing important happened. Does it matter?"

"It seems odd — driving around all day and never telling me anything about it."

She was suddenly furious with him for discussing it in front of Harriet and Robert. "Why? You don't give me a detailed account of your movements day by day."

"Isn't that rather different?"

"I can't see why. Is there one law for you and another for me?"

"You know that's not what I meant. I don't go off on pleasure trips without telling you anything about them."

"For heaven's sake, what does it matter? Your dinner was cooked when you got home, wasn't it? You weren't neglected."

"That's not the point."

"Then just what is the point?"

Harriet's amused voice, pretending to pour oil on troubled waters, interrupted them. "She only went for a little drive into the country, darling. If I'd my own car, do you think I wouldn't do the same?" When neither of them answered her, her mischievous eyes turned on Sarah. "Only I'm surprised at you picking up a hitch-hiker like that, darling. I didn't think any woman on her own did it these days, not after all the assaults one reads about. I know you're more trusting than I am, but just the same you ought to be more careful in the future."

They left the dance early and on their arrival home John brought up the affair again. Feeling enough had been said already she refused to discuss it any further with him, and he withdrew at once into one of his silent moods — worse ordeals than quarrels to her because of the time he could sustain them. When she found his mood unchanged the following morning, her first thought was that she had better change her plans for Wednesday in case he phoned Eunice, but then she remembered it was Michael's birthday. She was committing no crime — this time she was damned if she would capitulate.

Instead she waited until Tuesday and made her announcement just before dinner when he was reading the evening paper. "By the way, it's Miss Phillips' birthday tomorrow so I shall be spending the evening with her."

Although she saw he had stopped reading he did not answer her.

"Did you hear what I said? I shall be with the old lady tomorrow evening."

At that he lowered the paper. "What if you are? You're out every Wednesday evening in any case."

"I'm telling you so that if you phone Eunice again you'll know where I am. Also because I might be a little later than usual. She gets so few chances to talk to people it isn't always easy to get away."

He made an impatient exclamation. "If you didn't keep her locked away like a state secret she wouldn't be so starved of conversation. What are you afraid of — that we'll laugh at her?"

She tried to hide her dismay. "I've explained at least a dozen times — she's too self-conscious about her appearance."

"But not with you? What have you got that we haven't — a more sympathetic nature?"

She braced herself. "This is because I was seen with a man in my car last week, isn't it?"

"It's not because of anything. I'm just puzzled why you won't let me meet your friends occasionally."

"But I've just told you why — she would be embarrassed."

"I'm not just talking about her. What about Eunice and her husband — they're nearly as big a mystery."

She gave a helpless laugh. "I thought I was doing you a favour. Eunice is mad about classical music — I've known her chatter about it for hours. It would bore you as much as golf bores me."

"Meaning you find my friends boring?"

"Meaning nothing except that however close two people are, their personal tastes must differ sometimes. But does it matter?"

"It matters when friends start to think there's something wrong."

She stiffened. "What friends? Harriet?"

From the way his eyes avoided her, she knew her guess was right. "No more than anyone else, I shouldn't think. But it's obvious she's puzzled why you keep the old woman to yourself like this. Everybody knows that a person in that condition ought to be brought out as much as possible. And we're all willing to help."

She gave a laugh of anger. "Do you think Harriet cares anything about helping an old woman? All she cares about is making trouble. I don't want her in this house again, John. She sees every other woman as her enemy and spreads her poison about like her damned perfume."

"Don't talk rubbish. In any case, why blame her? From the way you keep your friends from us, anyone would think it odd."

"My friends! All two of them! What about all the people you play golf with? What about your business associates? I don't think there's anything queer going on when you spend an evening with them."

He flung his newspaper down and rose. "You can see my friends at any time and you know it. It's your fault that you don't, not mine. What is it — don't you like being seen out with me?"

She knew that only genuine distress would cause him to lose control like this, and her tone changed. "Don't exaggerate, please. How often does either of us go out without the other? One evening a week — twice if you happen to be playing golf. You know perfectly well it hasn't anything to do with my feelings for you — why on earth should it have?"

Looking as if about to make a bitter comment, he changed his mind and walked out of the room instead. Two minutes later she heard the side door slam as he went out to his car. When he did not arrive home by midnight she began wondering if he had gone to stay with friends but ten minutes after retiring

226

to bed she heard his car enter the drive.

She pretended to be asleep when he came upstairs. At first he lay motionless at the far side of the bed but just as she was resigning herself to another few days of silent reproach his hand touched her arm.

"Darling. Are you asleep?"

"No," she whispered. "What is it?"

He turned fully towards her. "I've had a wretched evening thinking about what happened, and I want to say how sorry I am. Only it hurts me somehow when you need other people — it makes me feel I'm failing you in some way. Can't you understand that?"

"Of course I understand. But I could just as well feel I'm letting you down by not playing golf. You're hurting yourself for nothing, darling."

"Perhaps I am. But you've a different nature to mine. You don't seem to get as jealous as I do."

"But you haven't any reason to be jealous. How many times must I keep telling you that?"

He drew her towards him and kissed her. Wanting a reconciliation herself, she offered no resistance but as he began making love to her she discovered to her horror there was a part of her that would not comply. When she tried to conceal it, her own love-making developed a feverishness that drew his attention. In the light of the street lamps outside, she could see his face above her, searching, anxious, vulnerable in his desire.

"You're sure there's nothing wrong, darling? Nothing I ought to know?"

She swallowed. "No. No, of course there isn't."

He made love to her as if trying to drive all thoughts of others from them both. She struggled to match his mood but could hide the truth from herself no longer. In the past she had lived with his possessiveness by avoiding situations that provoked it. Now, confronted by the choice between her conscience and her acquiescence, her love for him was becoming more desire than reality. She *wanted* to love him but the chains he used to hold her were inexorably pulling her away, and the knowledge brought a silent, aching grief.

16

SHE felt edgy and apprehensive when she went to the cottage on Wednesday. After nearly nine months of trouble-free visits she had, as she now realized, developed a false sense of security, and she found herself once again scrutinizing every car that passed her.

She had been wondering if Michael's novel had been returned yet from the publisher but his appearance as he opened the cottage door was reassuring: he was wearing his new clothes and a green tie she had not seen before.

"Happy birthday," she greeted him, giving his arm a squeeze and handing him a small parcel. "Here's a little present for you — I hope you like it."

The present was the Dictionary of Phrase and Fable and he looked pleased with it. "How did you guess I wanted this?"

"I once heard you say what a useful book it was. But tell me about the novel.

Have you had any news yet?"

"Not really. Only a letter from the editor saying it was a subject that interested them and they'd be glad to give the book careful consideration."

"But that's splendid news. It must help if they like the theme."

He gave a wry grimace. "I don't know. It still has to be good in its own right."

She wanted to chide him for his lack of optimism and yet knew it was better he did not build up too much hope. "It is good. Better than you think. I like that tie you're wearing. Is it a new one?"

"Yes. I bought it yesterday. The money for the serial arrived. That's something I want to talk about." He opened a drawer in the desk and pulled out a wad of notes. "Please take these. They're a little of what I owe you."

Her mind was not on the money. If he had bought the tie it must mean he'd found the courage to enter a men's outfitters. She counted the notes. "I can't take all this. There's ten pounds here."

"Why not? If everything you've given me were added up it would come to five times as much. Take it and I'll give you some more from my next sale."

"Won't you wait just a little longer?" she pleaded. "There are so many things you need."

The old, familiar sullenness began to tug at his mouth. "What's the matter? Don't you think I'm going to sell anything else?"

She took the warning and put the money in her handbag. "It's your birthday, so I won't argue if that's what you want. Did you buy the tie in Wareham?"

"Yes. I managed to get the motor bike going and took it in for servicing."

"It must have been fun to be able to do a little shopping," she said, watching him. "Did you buy anything else?"

From the way he bent down to pat the dog she knew he was aware of the significance of her questions. "One or two things. A raincoat and a pair of shoes."

She could no longer conceal her delight. "And it wasn't a bit difficult, was it? You've realized at last how stupid you've been these last few years."

He stiffened in protest, then went on patting the dog. She caught his arm playfully and shook him. "Are you listening? You've got this thing beaten now, haven't you? Come on — I want to hear you say it."

Her touch seemed like a catalyst. She heard his breath suck in, he straightened sharply, and before she could move his arms were around her and his lips hard against her own. For fully ten seconds his strength was almost punitive. Then, as abruptly, he released her and turned away. She saw his hands were clenched and that he was trembling. As she reached into her handbag for cigarettes, she heard his voice, gritty with self-hatred. "Sorry. That was bloody silly of me."

She tried to give him a cigarette but he pulled away. Her half-laugh was as much to control her own emotions as to bring relief to his. "All right, it was silly but let's make no more of it than that. What about dinner? Would you like it now or later?"

He kept his face from her as he moved towards the window. She waited a moment, then became impatient. "For heaven's sake, Michael, it's not the end of the world. I'm not holding it against you, so let's forget about it. Otherwise the evening's going to be ruined."

At that he accepted the cigarette. Feeling he was best left alone until he recovered she moved towards the kitchen. "I think I'll start preparing dinner. I've brought a small chicken, so it'll take a little time. Put the radio on, will you?"

After dinner they went out into the back garden. It was a mellow, late-summer evening with a red sun low behind the birch. The apples were almost ripe and windfalls lay among the tangled grass. From somewhere near by a jackdaw chattered like an angry woman. Then the heath was silent again, somnolent after its summer labours.

They stood on the path while Michael, still diffident, threw a stick for Robbie. As one of his arch-enemies, a squirrel, diverted the dog and sent him racing towards the fence, Michael glanced at her.

"Well, are we going out tonight or not?"

She tried to smile. "Do you want to?"

"You don't sound very keen."

"Of course I'm keen. But I don't mind

stopping in tonight if that's what you prefer."

"I don't get you sometimes," he muttered. "For months you've been nagging at me to go out — you gave me a lecture about it only an hour ago — and now when I suggest it you talk like this. What's changed your mind?"

His readiness to put the blame on his earlier behaviour if she showed any opposition was all too evident. She also wondered if, beneath his sullenness, there was not a desire to demonstrate to her his newly-found confidence.

"Nothing's changed my mind," she told him. "It's just that as it's your birthday I want to do as you please. Where shall we go?"

"I wanted you to choose. Isn't there any place you particularly like?"

"Not really. I'd rather leave it to you."

He shrugged. "Then how about going the other way for a change — perhaps into the New Forest. I've only been through it a couple of times. Or do you prefer to keep well away from Bournemouth?"

She hid her apprehension well. "No, if we stay around Lyndhurst it should be all right. And there are some lovely pubs there. What about Robbie? Are you bringing him with us?"

"I don't think so. He'll be all right here for a couple of hours."

She never knew what instinct made her drive her car into the rear courtyard of the Green Man, for there was plenty of room in the front car park when they arrived. Inside they found a table alongside the fireplace where a log fire was burning. It had been newly-lit and the smoke gave the room the nostalgic smell of late summer.

With the holiday season not yet over the room was well filled but by insisting on buying the first round of drinks and then keeping Michael occupied in conversation about his work, she succeeded in easing his early embarrassment. With the subjugation of the scar his mood began to change, and after a second drink he was gayer than she had ever known him. It seemed that at last his mind was accepting the defeat of the tyranny that had oppressed it so long and the relief was an intoxication in itself.

Watching him and thinking of the twisted, embittered man she had met nine months ago, she experienced a happiness both rare and exquisite. She knew the cause and by the time she had drunk a few martinis she was in no mood for self-effacement. In part this man was her creation: from the broken clay that life had tossed aside she had helped mould this new being who could laugh and live again. Her joy rivalled the joy of the creative artist who found his work a success.

That such an act of creation between two people could have a more profound significance she was not aware at that moment. All she knew was that her senses seemed to have acquired a new awareness. The logs burned with a richer flame, the aroma of the woodsmoke was almost poignantly nostalgic, the brass that winked genially from the walls gave the room an exquisite cosiness. What was it her old Yorkshire grandfather, a philosopher if there had ever been one, had once said to her?

'Life's like a long walk through a desert, lassie. Sand and heat and thirst, and then you come to an oasis. No one's allowed many of 'em, so when you reach one don't do as most people do and start worrying about the next stretch ahead. Drink the cool water, eat the figs and dates, roll over in the cool grass. Give it your mind as well as your body — enjoy the colours, the scents, the sound of the leaves. Give yourself to every minute of it, lassie — there's no other way to live.'

She was obeying the old man tonight, she thought, as another martini turned warm inside her. This was an oasis that was the richer for the stony haul before it. Her only shivers of reality came when newcomers entered the room but when she recognized none of them her confidence grew that nothing would disturb this evening. Even when memory, like a treacherous draught, reminded her of her shattered optimism the previous Friday she turned it into comfort that the same ill luck could hardly befall her twice in so short a time.

Outside, through the wide, uncurtained window, the fading twilight could be seen. When Michael, his face flushed from unaccustomed alcohol, asked her to have yet another martini she succumbed on a wave of recklessness.

"Yes, all right. Only it'll have to be the last — we've quite a long drive back."

He nodded and went to the bar. As she watched him with affection a movement in the car park outside caught her eye and she saw a car was pulling up opposite the window. In spite of the fading light and reflections in the glass she recognized the car as a 1961 Morris and a faint jab of alarm stiffened her — Robert had a Morris of the same vintage. Robert's was dark blue — this one's colour was hidden by the twilight.

Doors opened and slammed closed. The men moved straight towards the pub entrance, giving her no chance to identify them. The women, however, waited a moment to exchange some confidence before walking past the window. One was stout and matronly, the other small and neat with the light stride of a kitten. The dusk hid their features but as Sarah watched in hypnotic fascination the smaller woman paused to glance into the room and the light fell on her face. The girl's heart seemed to stop, then gave an explosive thud as she recognized Harriet. Paralysed for a moment she saw Harriet's eyes travel round the room, pass her table, then suddenly jerk back. As they widened in surprise and excitement, Sarah leapt to her feet and ran towards Michael who was returning from the bar. Beer from the glass he was holding spilled out and ran down her costume as she caught his arm.

"Michael, we have to leave. I'm sorry but it's urgent. Please come — quickly."

Sensitive as he was, her fear communicated itself to him immediately. "What's happened? Is it someone you know?"

Making him put the glasses down on a table she half-dragged him towards a side door. "There's no time now. I'll explain later."

The door led into a narrow passage. The front entrance was on their left. Robert and his brother must have gone into a smaller bar on the opposite side. Expecting Harriet to appear at any moment Sarah turned from the entrance and ran down the passage. At the far end other passages branched off both left and right. A moment of agonized indecision and she took the one on the left. She ran past a private lounge and came to a closed door. It opened as she tugged at it and as cold air touched her face she discovered with immense relief that she was in the rear courtyard.

She had forgotten Michael's disability and had to wait painful seconds until he caught up with her. "Wait here," she panted. "I'll bring the car over."

Breathless and trembling by the time she reached the car, she wasted more time fumbling in her handbag for the keys. Finding Michael alongside her she flung open his door and started up the engine.

The rest was pure nightmare. She was certain Harriet's ferret-sharp brain would see at once where her only escape route lay, and as she approached the exit of the courtyard she had a vision of Harriet running up to the car window. What she would do, with Michael as sensitive as a fused bomb alongside her, she did not know, although it was obvious that if she drove straight past Harriet her guilt would seem proven.

The absurd idea, panic-induced, that

the car might escape unrecognized made her drive out on side-lights only. She dared not look left or right and the time it took the car to clear the exit seemed interminable. Even when they were out on the road she could not believe she had escaped a confrontation. Driving as fast as the winding road would permit, chased by the ridiculous fear Harriet would make Robert follow her, she needed a glimpse of Michael's face to pull herself together. Slowing down, she turned to him.

"I'm sorry. But when I saw them drive up it seemed the only thing to do."

"Who was it?" he muttered. "Your husband?"

She realized it was what he would think. "No. It was some friends of ours. At least the woman's supposed to be a friend but I know I can't trust her."

"Did she see you?"

"I'm afraid so." Her mind shivered into panic again at the memory of Harriet's face. What would the bitch do now? Phone John? Or play a cat-and-mouse game for a while?

Michael had turned sharply away. "So

it's over? You won't be able to see me again."

Afraid for him and badly needing comfort herself, she fumbled for his hand. "Things mightn't turn out as badly as we think. So let's try not to get too upset."

For a moment their hands clung together. Then with a curse, he tore away. "Not be upset! From the way you acted back there the devil himself might have been after you. What have you got for a husband — a sadist?"

The road was narrow and winding. Feeling unable to contend with it while he was in this mood, she pulled on to the verge and switched off the engine.

"I got a shock because to see you tonight I had to tell John I was visiting someone else. If he finds out I've spent the evening in a pub with an unknown man I can hardly blame him if he gets the wrong ideas."

The scar was a huge brand across his face and he moved about in his seat as if in physical pain. "For Christ's sake, why didn't you tell me things were as bad as this? If I'd known I'd never have let you go on seeing me."

His reaction was worse for her because she understood it. Wanting her to be free and having never seen her husband or friends, he had subconsciously submerged all the unwelcome facts of her private life to a depth where they seemed unreal and certainly negotiable. Tonight's evidence that their friendship was perilously insecure had come as a brutal shock.

"Don't exaggerate things," she pleaded. "I know I shouldn't have lost my head like that but I didn't want him to catch me out in a lie. Or to think things that have never happened. Surely you can understand that?"

His change of tone frightened her. "You've been using me as a diversion, haven't you? Someone to fool around and experiment with until your husband came home in the evenings."

"That's unfair — I've worried myself sick about you. But you can't blame me for being married and you can't blame John for becoming suspicious if he finds out I've been lying to him."

"I suppose you're going to tell me next that he loves you."

"He does. Very much."

His harsh laugh mocked her. "He loves you but you can't have a male friend without having to lie and run out of the back doors of pubs! Let's hope he never hates you or you'll be in real trouble."

Her resentment turned on him. Why did the ungrateful fool punish her for things beyond her control?

"You attack him for being jealous but are you so certain you're free of it? Sometimes I think you're not."

His head jerked round and in the semi-darkness she saw his bleak, condemning eyes. "When have I asked anything of you? Tell me that?"

When she did not answer he turned away, his bitterness turning into the abstract thing it had been when they first met. "What sort of a lousy world is it when two people feel guilty for going into a pub for a talk? When they have to run like criminals when a 'friend' sees them? I was right all along — it is hell out there. And you've nagged and nagged at me for months to get back into it. Why couldn't you leave me alone? I'd got it licked before you came — it couldn't hurt any more."

Tears were suddenly blinding her. "It was an awful thing to happen, I know. But there's no reason why it should affect your life. For my sake, don't go to pieces and spoil everything now."

All at once his fear was an exposed wound. "What does that mean? Goodbye?"

"How can I say anything at the moment? But at least you've got your confidence back. If you keep on going out like this you'll soon have plenty of friends."

He looked as if she had stabbed him. "Christ, I was right about you, wasn't I? The sick animal's better, so let it go — it'll soon find plenty of its own kind out there in the fields. You callous bitch. I'd rather have those indifferent bastards out there than hypocrites like you."

She sat white and mute as his agonized voice lashed out at her. At one moment her mind was crying in sympathy, in the next it was occupied with Harriet. Had she phoned home yet? Was John waiting up to see her? Oh God, make him stop. Let him think of me for a moment.

It was well past ten o'clock when they reached the cottage and another fifteen minutes before she dared to leave him. At the door she turned back. "You will take care of yourself until I see you again, won't you?"

He was sitting slumped in front of the oil heater. His stricken eyes lifted. "I thought you weren't coming here again."

"You know I shall come. But I can't say when until I know what's happened." When he did not speak she appealed to him again. "Promise to look after yourself, Michael, please."

"Give me one reason why I should," he said bitterly.

Her anger came back. Had he learned this was another way to hurt her? "Can't you do this one thing for me? I'm suffering too, you know — I'm the one who's in trouble tonight."

Shame made him turn away. "I'll eat and work and sleep if that's what you want. I haven't much choice, have I?"

It had to suffice. "And remember your promise — if you get any news about your book before you see me again, write me at the GPO, Bournemouth. I shall go in

246

this Saturday and next Tuesday to see if there's a letter."

Her last anxious glance showed him huddled over the oil heater, his face stained red in its glow. Outside it had turned cold as if the first breath of autumn had arrived and dried leaves rustled as she went down the path to her car.

17

SHE arrived home a few minutes after eleven and her first impression was that John was ignorant of the night's happenings. The sitting-room lights were shaded — the usual indication he was watching television — and the side door of the house remained closed as she drove into the garage.

She sat a moment in the darkness. She knew that even if Harriet had not got in touch with him yet, her correct move was to make a clean breast of everything. But it was a decision easier to make than to perform. There was so much that was difficult to explain, so much that needed both trust and imagination. If she had believed John lacked those qualities before there was little justification for hoping they would be in evidence tonight.

It took an effort of will to leave the car and make for the side door. As she paused before it, latch-key in hand, she heard the distant cry of a nightbird and a personal loneliness she had felt when in the car with Michael came back.

The hall was dimly lit: she paused outside the sitting-room door for a moment and then, conscious of her procrastination, went into the cloakroom where she examined her appearance in the mirror. She looked pale and there was a thinness about her cheeks she had not noticed before.

The relief she found in this respite now turned into uneasiness. John must surely have heard her car unless the television was turned on loud and yet there had been no sound of it in the hall. Returning to the sitting-room door she discovered she was right: the room was silent. About to enter it, she heard the study door behind her open and turning sharply saw John in the doorway.

He was fully dressed and she knew at once he had heard from Harriet. His expression contained more than outrage, however — his cheeks were pale and his eyes drawn. Alcohol ... distress ... whatever the cause her defences were suddenly outflanked. If she could be tolerant to Michael for his darker, embittered self, should she not be equally tolerant to John for his possessiveness? Was he not, if less dramatically, also a victim of his environment? Whatever pain he caused her, whatever misconceptions he laboured under, John suffered to — the evidence was on his face tonight.

Her voice was perilously unsteady. "John, there's something I have to tell you. Will you come into the sitting-room?"

She could almost feel him working up his anger. "What am I going to get this time? More lies or the truth at last?"

She made herself look straight at him. "Did Harriet phone you or did she come round?"

"She phoned. Robert didn't want her to but she felt you might need help. If you hadn't run away it might have been different."

It was difficult to talk about Harriet without every word holding an overtone of hate. "What exactly did she say?"

"She said she and Robert and those relatives of theirs went for a drive tonight and called at a pub called The Green Man. As they got out of the car she saw you through a window. You must have seen her at the same time because you jumped up in fright and ran towards the bar. There was a man there; you grabbed his arm and ran out with him through the rear of the pub. A minute later you drove out of the car park and went tearing down the road as if half the police in Hampshire were after you."

"And what did Harriet make of that?"

"What would anyone make of it? She didn't want me to know but felt for your sake I should in case you were in some kind of trouble."

Oh, God, she thought; you can't believe that of Harriet. All the way home she had told herself that however justifiable her conduct might seem to her, any man without the full facts would find it suspicious, and she owed John every patience. For the moment, however, her aversion of Harriet was dominant.

"Her duty as a friend, I suppose?"

He needed nothing more to trigger off his anger. "Don't blame Harriet for what's happened. And don't look as if you've been wronged either. You've been telling me a pack of lies for months: you've even told me you were visiting a sick, old woman who was afraid of meeting people." His voice choked, whether from anger or distress it was impossible to say. "What a hell of a thing to do — to let people think you were being kind when you were having an affair instead."

She took warning from her own anger. Real guilt could endure accusations. The justification that she felt was less durable.

"Please don't say any more until you've heard everything," she said quietly. "My lie about the old woman wasn't as bad as it sounds — not when you've heard my reason for it."

"Then there isn't an old woman!" He looked more shocked than triumphant. "What about Eunice? Have you been using her as a cover too?"

"No. At least not in the way you think. Come into the sitting-room. I want to tell you everything and we may as well talk like civilized people."

"Even if we don't act like them." Pain made him spiteful. "What do you want — time to think up more lies?"

A single wave of temper broke from her and shivered into words. "John, the only thing you have against me so far is a malicious phone call from Harriet. If you prejudge me because of her, if you don't give me a fair chance to explain, I shall leave this house and never come back. I mean it, so make up your mind."

He cursed, crossed the hall, and pushed open the sitting-room door. "All right. Go in there if you think it'll help you to explain things any better."

She bent down a moment before the fire, holding out her chilled hands. There was little warmth, the log embers had long turned grey. Rising, she offered him a cigarette. His first reaction was a curt headshake, then, as if thinking the refusal too childish, he took it and gave her a light.

"Well, I'm waiting. You've admitted you've lied about the old woman and you've as good as admitted you were in a pub tonight with a man. So now I'd like you to fill in the details."

"It's the details that make all the difference, John. Will you try to understand them and not write them off as excuses?"

He inhaled smoke. "I'm asking to hear them, aren't I? Whether they're excuses or not, I'll decide for myself."

Fighting back a sense of hopelessness she dropped into an armchair. "Do you remember my coming home one afternoon last year and telling you my car had broken down?"

He nodded. "Yes. You said a man in a cottage had fixed it." Then he gave a start. "Is this the same man?"

"It's the man Harriet saw me with tonight, yes."

"But that was last November. Are you saying you've been going with him all this time?"

"Give me a chance, John. It wasn't the way you think. He was dressed almost in rags and so poor he couldn't afford fuel to warm the cottage. More than that, he wasn't well — he'd had a bad accident two years earlier that had cost him his wife and his job. It had hurt him so much he was like a wounded animal, snarling at anyone who came near." She went on, trying to explain Michael's obsession over his appearance. "It's a psychological thing and it was crippling him — it wouldn't let him leave the cottage and he was trying to make a living writing short stories. But it was obvious he'd never succeed on his own — he needed someone to talk to, to read his work, to reassure him about his appearance. I did what I had to do, John. There was no-one else to help him."

His laugh was one of pure disbelief. "A neurotic writer with a persecution mania — an unsung genius living in a hovel . . . In God's name what are you giving me?"

"I'm not giving you anything. This is exactly how it happened."

"How old is he?" he demanded.

"I don't know. Twenty-seven or twenty-eight — I've never asked."

His jealousy was suddenly too corrosive an acid to contain. "Oh, I'm with you now. The sick, young Bohemian in his den — they say it never fails with women. And you always were a Romantic."

Her white face stared at him. "You've already made up your mind I've been having an affair with him, haven't you?"

"Are you denying it?"

"Yes, I am. I'm bitterly denying it. All I've done is visit him once a week so that he's had someone to talk to. What's so shameful about that?"

He gave another incredulous laugh. "You never say a word about him to me: you make up a pack of fantastic lies about an old school teacher who's had a stroke: you pile deception upon deception and when you're at last found out you ask me what's shameful about it. Has he turned your head? Don't you know right from wrong any more?"

She leaned forward in her chair, her voice was very quiet. "John. Do you remember Mr Branson?"

He gave a faint start. "What about Branson?"

"I think you know. I was honest about him, John. I told you everything and I brought him home to meet you. And what happened? You made it one of the most uncomfortable evenings of my life. You even teased me in front of that bitch Harriet that you'd met my latest boy friend. But worst of all you made it impossible for me to help him again."

His face was sullen again. "How do you make that out?"

"Because you gave him the message. She's married — she's mine. Keep off! I wasn't allowed to give friendship to a lonely, little man who'd buried his mother only the previous week. Someone I hardly thought of as a man at all but only a person in trouble. It's been that way for seven years, John."

"Been like what for seven years?"

"You know what I mean. I didn't want to help Michael without telling you — I've hated and resented every lie I've had to make, particularly as I was afraid this might happen. But what choice have you given me?"

"In other words it's my fault that you've told all these lies?"

She met his gaze squarely. "Yes, it is. By being so possessive. But that's as far as it's gone. Whatever that bitch Harriet made you think, I've never been unfaithful to you in my life."

He started to speak, then drew on his cigarette. In the silence, beneath his resentment, she could feel his desire to believe her. Outside a car drove past, its headlights glowing for a moment through the closed curtains. He sucked in smoke again, then turned back to her.

"Is he on the telephone?"

She shook her head. "He can't afford one."

"All right, then what's his address. I'll run out tomorrow and see him."

Although she had been expecting it she gave a start of dismay. "No, you can't do that. He's upset as it is by what happened tonight. If you go out there asking if we've been sleeping together you might set him back where he was a year ago."

"For God's sake, I'm not going to be as crude as that. I only want a short talk with him. He knows you're married, doesn't he?"

"Yes, of course. But I've been trying to win back his faith. If he thinks I've sold him out for my own protection he might go completely to pieces."

"That's ridiculous. Pure melodrama. If he's a real friend he'll be only too glad to clear things up between us."

She gave a laugh of despair. "You see — you're incapable of understanding people like him. Their minds are raw, bleeding — they've been hurt so much they're looking for treachery everywhere. If he loses faith in me it could destroy him."

He looked as if all his earlier suspicions were back.

"Don't you think it's time you spared a thought for my feelings? I haven't had the happiest of nights thinking of you sleeping with another man. I want his address. Otherwise don't blame me for the conclusions I draw."

"You're asking me to sell him for my own protection. Can't you see that?"

"No. I'm asking it for the sake of our marriage. For you and me."

She was trembling. "Don't ask me, John. Please don't ask me."

18

HE looked as uncompromising as she had ever seen him. "I want his address. I've a right to it and I want it."

She had a mental picture of him knocking on the cottage door. 'There's a strong rumour going around that you and my wife are having an affair. She denies it but she's given me your address to put my mind at rest. Do you mind if I come in?'

Her mind shrank from the vision. "I want to give it, John, but I can't."

"And yet you still expect me to believe you?"

"Is that so much to ask of one's husband?"

"Is it so surprising I find it difficult after all that's happened?"

No, she thought, it wasn't surprising. Jealousy leading to lies . . . lies leading to jealousy . . . round and round the circle you went until you hardly knew right from wrong.

His suspicions were in full flood again. "Why are you protecting him like this? Say what you like, you're acting as if the two of you were in love."

Put like that, she thought, he made love sound like a dirty word. "What exactly does love mean to you, John? You don't ask me if I'm in love with him — you *accuse* me of it."

"What are you getting at now?"

"I'm saying that compassion, affection, any feeling of warmth or concern I might get for another man is always associated with sex in your mind. Do you believe one has to feel sex before one can feel charity? Do you believe our sexual organs are the seat of our conscience?"

"For God's sake, stop talking rubbish."

"I'm not talking rubbish. We've got our values wrong: we've made a tyrant out of sex. If it inhibits us so much we have to stop acting like decent human beings, then it's being taken too seriously. We're putting too high a price on it."

"What are you trying to sell me now? Free love?"

"I'm not trying to sell you anything," she said bitterly. "But to me it's a cold and shoddy world if every time we see someone of the opposite sex needing help we have to draw back in case we get our fingers burned."

"No-one suggested you do that. All that's asked is that you bring your husband into it. Is that so unreasonable?"

"But what if one can't, as in this case? What then?"

"Then you put your marriage first. If you value it, that is."

"In other words you sell your conscience for it?"

His control seemed to snap. "Stop talking like that. For God's sake, what's all this leading up to? That you have slept with him?"

She felt a desire to punish him. "You won't believe me, will you? So what would you do if I said yes? Would you forgive me?"

As he lifted his cigarette she saw his hands were trembling. "I wonder if you'd find forgiveness so easy if I was unfaithful to you."

"Perhaps I wouldn't. But at least I'd learn that nobody owns anybody else — that we're not possessions like our houses and our cars."

He nodded bitterly. "Harriet once asked me where you were getting your trendy new ideas from. It's obvious enough now. Are you going to give me his address or not?"

"I can't, John. I've just told you why."

"Even though I can't get my trust back until the whole thing's out in the open? If he's as neurotic as you say, I'll promise I'll do nothing to upset him. But for the sake of our marriage, give me his address."

The silence that followed seemed deep enough to drown in. "You're asking me to sell him for my own protection, John. And I can't do it."

His eyes, suffused with condemnation and pain, held her for a long moment before he turned and made for the door. Apprehensive and yet with the absurd desire to comfort him, she was following when the door slammed closed between them.

He slept in the guest room that night and in the immediate days that followed she saw little of him. On both Thursday and Friday he phoned from work to say he would not be home for dinner, always with an excuse and yet with a sullen defiance that made his real reason clear. On Saturday afternoon he visited a friend and on Sunday he hardly left his room all day. Such meals as they had together were ordeals of silence or monosyllabic requests. It was behaviour he seemed able to sustain indefinitely but it was torment to her.

In addition she was worried about Michael. Not knowing what had happened to her and with his highly-developed imagination at work, he could well be suffering more than she was. She wanted to write him, but knowing that in his hypersensitive condition a badly-phrased sentence could trigger off a host of adverse reactions, she found it difficult to fill the wide expanse of notepaper with the right assurances. Eventually, feeling its brevity was a safeguard, she sent him a postcard, assuring him there was nothing to worry about and that she would visit him at her first opportunity.

When John went unexpectedly to the office on Saturday morning, she took the opportunity to slip out to the central post office. There was no letter awaiting her and although she knew this could mean anything or nothing her sense of uneasiness grew until she decided to risk a visit to the cottage on Monday morning.

Thinking it was wiser to be home by the early afternoon in case John phoned, she left only a few minutes after he drove off to the office. The harvest was in and beyond Upton starlings and crows were busy on the stripped fields. The summer traffic had all but disappeared although there was a small Morris saloon behind her as she dipped down the shallow hill to the cottage. She slowed down and waited until it had gone past before turning into the garden.

Michael was at the door before she switched off the engine. He was wearing his old clothes and his hollow cheeks convinced her he had lost more weight. He could not hide his relief at seeing her and she gave his arm an affectionate squeeze.

"Hello. As there wasn't a letter for me I thought I'd drive out for a couple of hours. I take it there's no news yet about the novel?"

She noticed him pause before he followed her into the sitting room. Trying to calm the ebullient Robbie, who was leaping up at her, she turned to him. "What is it? Have you heard something?"

He gave a cynical grin. "Yes. It came back on Saturday."

She felt almost sick. "What did they say?"

"What didn't they say? Chuck it up and become a farm labourer that's what it more or less boiled down to. But never mind about that. What's happened at home?"

She was not deceived. Already haunted that he might lose her companionship, he could not have received the news at a worse time. He looked ill and there was an air of abandonment about him that frightened her.

She knew she had to play everything down. "Nothing much. I've had a long chat with John and explained everything. He hasn't quite accepted it yet but he will in time."

Although it was news he must have been expecting, his increased pallor told her it still came as a shock. "Did you tell him yourself or had he heard about us from that woman?"

"Harriet phoned before I got home," she admitted.

"Jesus Christ. And you say she's a friend of yours?"

"Yes. We used to see them once a fortnight, sometimes once a week."

The scar was crawling back over his face. "It's great out there, isn't it? Full of goodwill and charity. Come on, she says — get back into it and start living again. So what happens now?"

"Nothing happens. I just have to be a little careful for a time, that's all."

"But you said you'd told him about me?"

"I have. But I didn't give him your name or address."

Behind his searching eyes she saw his relief. "Why not?"

"I don't really know," she lied.

"What did you tell him about me — that I was a drop-out you'd taken pity on?"

She turned away. "I told the truth — that I'd met someone who was lonely

267

and needed a friend."

"But you had to give another reason. You had to tell him I was a twisted freak or he'd never have believed you weren't having an affair."

She closed her eyes. "I told him nothing I haven't told you. I said you had a stupid obsession about your appearance that had prevented your going out and meeting people. That was all."

The self-destructive elements in him were suddenly naked. "And I'm supposed to believe a possessive bastard like your John will believe that. Why haven't you the guts to admit what you really said about me?"

Goaded beyond control by his masochism, she swung round on him. "All right, if you want the truth, here it is. He doesn't believe I haven't had an affair and he won't believe it until I've given him your name and address. Does that satisfy you?"

His eyes widened with shock. To hide it he gave a jeering laugh. "I get it now. You really came out this morning to ask me to see him."

They're flogging me to hide their own

frailties, she thought, hating them both at that moment. "No. I came out because I thought you'd be worried about what was happening. The last thing I want is the two of you to meet."

His shame was now as palpable as his bitterness. "But if he won't believe you, what's going to happen now?"

"I don't know," she said quietly. "I'll just have to wait and see, won't I?"

He muttered something and moved across to the window. As the dog whined uneasily he spoke without turning his head. "You'd better arrange a meeting then. Give him my address and fix a time."

For a few seconds she was full of hope. Perhaps she had underestimated the extent of his recovery. A small thing made her hesitate: a nerve was twitching at the base of his jaw.

"Where would you see him? Here?"

The nerve seemed to quicken. "I suppose so. Then he can see that everything else you must have told him is true."

She drew closer, trying to see his expression. "You know what I'm afraid of, don't you? Could you talk to him without losing your temper?"

There was a brief, tight silence. Then: "I don't know. But I can try, can't I?"

She was close enough now to see the shine on his forehead. "Why don't you want to meet him, Michael? Will you tell me?"

At that he turned. The disfiguring scar gave him a desperate appearance. "I don't know. Perhaps because I can't help feeling guilty."

"Guilty?"

"Why not? You've had to lie to come and see me. And it's been going on for nearly a year." His gesture was one of pure hatred. "That's what that bloody place out there does to you — it smears you with its own muck until you feel filthy too."

"And that's all?"

His eyes avoided her again. "Christ knows. Stop asking me fool questions. I said I'd see him, so arrange it and let's get it over."

She moved up to him, turned his face with her hand, and kissed his cheek. "Thank you for offering," she whispered.

"I know how hard it would have been for you. Now stop thinking about it because I shan't let it happen."

Her kiss seemed to have turned his face even paler and she could see tiny images of herself in his eyes. "You've been good to me, Sarah," he muttered. "I can't let you pay for it."

One thought stood out above all others — it was the first time he had called her by her name. She took his hand and pressed it. "I've already told him I won't give him your address and I shan't change my mind. So don't think or worry about it any more."

It was nearly three o'clock before she arrived home, two hours later than she had intended. She felt unnaturally tired but although she went to her room an uneasy feeling that John might have phoned would not let her rest. It grew until she found herself phoning him. Her excuse was an electric fire he had dropped in for repair the previous Tuesday and not yet collected. His secretary, Miss McIntosh, took her call.

"Oh, hello, Mrs Ashley. No, I'm sorry your husband isn't in. He went out just before noon and hasn't got back yet."

"Did he go out on business or was he going to lunch?"

"I think it must have been business, although I didn't know the gentleman he went with."

"Then he didn't say where he was going?"

Her insistence brought the slight but unmistakable reproach the secretary gives the prying wife. "No, Mrs Ashley. I think it must have been a private appointment. Shall I ask him to phone you when he comes in?"

"Yes, please, I'd like to catch him before he leaves for home."

Five o'clock came and she still had no call from John. Just before the office closed at five-thirty she spoke to the secretary again. "Isn't he back yet?"

"I'm sorry, Mrs Ashley, but I haven't seen him since lunch time."

"You mean he hasn't phoned you? What will you do?"

"I'll stay on for a while in case he comes back here. If he doesn't, perhaps you'll tell him I've locked up the office and taken his desk keys home."

She had a presentiment as sharp as a septic tooth as she lowered the receiver. John was far too ambitious and conscientious to leave the office for a whole afternoon without making advance arrangements. Something out of the ordinary had happened; of that she was certain.

Outside a rising wind was stirring the trees and littering the lawns with leaves. The sun was well down before she heard a car turning into the drive. Running to the sitting-room window she caught a glimpse of it before it vanished round the side of the house. Her face showed strain as she turned away. He had brought his mother with him — surely not to help him obtain Michael's address?

Sick at the prospect of yet another ordeal she waited by the door. As they entered the hall his mother made a comment she could not discern. A moment later John called out for her.

"Sarah, where are you? Mother's here."

She swallowed once, then walked out into the hall. "Hello, Mother. I wasn't expecting you. Have you ... ?" Her voice faded at John's appearance. Flushed and ill at ease, he gave his mother a glance that appeared a signal: she laid a bouquet of flowers on a hall chair and moved towards the sitting room. As she disappeared inside he turned to her with embarrassment.

"Sorry I'm late, darling. I've been out today and didn't get a chance to phone you."

When she did not answer he reached out and drew her towards him. "Do you think if I apologize you can forgive me? I've realized this afternoon what a fool I've been."

19

SHE was too overcome to do anything but press against him. He gave an ashamed laugh. "You were right in the things you said last Wednesday — I have been too jealous. Only this time I honestly thought there was something to be jealous about."

He reached down for the bouquet and handed it to her. Her eyes were wet as she stared through the cellophane at the red carnations. He gave a rueful grimace as her face lifted again. "Yes, it's a peace offering. The least I can give you."

She tried to pull herself together. "How much does your mother know?"

Mrs Ashley's masculine voice made both of them turn. "Everything, dear — John came to me last Thursday evening. I told him then it was absurd — you preferring some down-and-out scribbler — but he wouldn't be comforted. I wonder if you realize how lucky you are to have a man so jealous of you after all these years."

His mother was the last ally she expected. "I know how bad it looked but it did happen just as I said. I've probably been stupid; and yet I don't think anyone could have seen him as I did and not done something to help."

"I believe you, dear. But it was silly of you not to give John his address. That was asking for trouble."

With her senses numbed by reaction, the girl had no other wish but to appease. "I know how it must seem, but he's embittered to an abnormal degree. It's taken me all this time to gain his trust and I'm the only friend he has. If I'd let John go round he would think I'd betrayed him and there's no telling what the effect on him would be."

To her surprise John turned sharply away. As she glanced back at his mother she saw the woman's pale eyes held traces of defiance and embarrassment. Suddenly her presentiment was back.

"What's the matter?"

Neither answered her. The house seemed unnaturally quiet.

"What is it?" She swung back to John.

"There's something you haven't told me, isn't there?"

The mother was stronger than the son. "I want you to keep calm for a moment, dear, and listen to me. This wretched affair couldn't be allowed to go on — it would have been a tragedy for you and John to have lost faith in one another, perhaps even separated, over a misunderstanding. The only sensible thing to do was meet this young man and prove to John you were telling the truth."

"I don't understand. What are you telling me?"

"I'm telling you we've just seen him and both of us are now convinced you've not been having an affair."

Sarah looked stunned. "How could you? I haven't even given John his name."

Defiance hardened the woman's expression. "There are ways of getting information if the need is great enough. And this is a case where I'm certain the end justifies the means."

"Are you saying you've had someone follow me?" The girl was staring at John in disbelief.

Mrs Ashley moved quickly out of the doorway to his rescue. "You needn't blame John — the idea was mine. I wasn't prepared to stand by and see the poor boy worry himself sick with uncertainty. You admitted telling him falsehoods before — how could he be sure you weren't telling him another?"

As the truth sank in, the girl gave a violent start. "What happened? What did Michael say?"

John's face betrayed an agony of shame. "I'm sorry, darling. But I had to know one way or the other — I'd have gone crazy otherwise."

Her voice rose hysterically and struck at him. "I asked what happened."

"Nothing very much. It didn't take long to see you'd told me the truth. We can't have been in his place more than a few minutes."

She flung the bouquet of carnations to the floor. "So this is why I got the peace offering. What did you tell him? That you love me so much you pay spies to keep a watch on me?"

Once again Mrs Ashley answered for him. "We didn't get much of a chance to tell him anything. He went off like a lunatic when we said who we were. His language was so appalling that at one time I thought John was going to strike him."

The girl's nails dug into the palms of her hands. "What exactly was said? Please tell me everything."

"I can't remember it all — it was too dreadful. But at least it convinced us you had been telling the truth. As I told John, a girl like you couldn't possibly have had an affair with anyone so unprepossessing and vulgar. It stood out a mile you'd been seeing him only out of pity."

She felt the blood leave her face. "You didn't say this in front of him?"

"I don't know when I said it. It was a dreadful few minutes — something I wouldn't like to experience again. He didn't only abuse us — the ungrateful creature attacked you too. It's quite obvious he's psychopathic and needs medical attention."

Let me wake up and find this is a nightmare, she prayed. "You couldn't have done anything worse to him. Damn you — I'm the only one he trusted."

John was looking pale and shaken. "I agree it was a mistake. Only how could we know he was so unbalanced?"

The look she gave him made him flinch. As she ran into the cloakroom for a coat he followed her. "Where are you going?"

She shrank away from him. "Where do you think? God knows what you've done to him — it might have been kinder to stab him."

Again he tried to stop her. Pushing him away she ran down the hall, with Mrs Ashley's alarmed voice following her.

"Sarah, you mustn't see him alone. Not now. It might be dangerous. Sarah, you've no right to go. Not if John forbids it."

She turned in the doorway. "This is the last time he forbids me anything. Don't try to follow me, you, John, or your damned spy. If you do, you can be certain you'll never see me here again."

She had never driven so fast before and at times the wind made it difficult for her to control the car. In the suburbs it was severe enough, beyond Upton it was a wild thing, rampaging across the fields and tearing at the trees. The western sky was aflame but dusk lay like mist in the hollows and hedges.

As she drove she tried to prepare words for the ordeal ahead, but thinking meant remembering what had happened and that made her mind disintegrate. She could imagine no calculated act of cruelty likely to do Michael more harm and in her haste to reach him she took chances that at any other time would have horrified her.

She turned off the main road into the forest, broke out on to the heath, and was almost at the cottage before she braked, catching the uncut hedge with her side window as she swung into the front garden.

The loud rat-tat as she swung down the rusted knocker gave back a hollow sound. She waited no more than five seconds before hammering at the door again. This time she put her ear to it but could hear no sound or answering bark from the dog.

Running round the side of the cottage with the idea of forcing a way through the bushes to the back door she saw the motor cycle was missing. Fighting back panic, she tried to think where he could have gone. Nowhere where there were people, he would avoid them like a wounded animal. She could think of only one place — the cliffs near St Albans. Since his recent sale she knew he had started going there again. Without an alternative it was a possibility she dared not overlook and she ran back to her car.

She remembered little of that ride except the buffeting of the wind and the squeal of the tyres. Her mind was ahead of her, searching the high cliffs. She missed the gravel road in the dusk and had to search back for it, every extra second hammering its loss into her mind. Finding it at last she accelerated round the hill, her spinning tyres throwing out showers of loose gravel. Driving as far past the stone quarry as she could, she jumped out of the car and made for the cliffs on foot.

As the quarry disappeared and the dusk-shadowed hillside opened out ahead, her run slowed down to a walk. At the best it had been only a possibility; now she felt her choice had been governed more by fear than by reason. Had she been able to think of any other likely place she would probably have turned back. As it was, she went on with a growing sense of hopelessness.

As she approached the first stile a bulky object, half-hidden in the hedge, changed her mood. It was a motor cycle, and although she did not know the make of Michael's machine, the wicker basket over the rear wheel, suitable for carrying a small animal, started her heart pounding again.

Climbing over the stile she ran towards the cliffs. The wind became stronger as she left the lee of the hills and made her stumble in the long grass. As she neared the cliffs the entire canopy of sky became visible, black except for a single slash of crimson over the sea.

She was struggling for breath when she reached the path that ran along the cliff edge. On both sides of her the headlands marched away into the gathering darkness. Hesitating, she ran in the direction they had taken on their first outing together.

After a few minutes two familiar headlands appeared out of the gloom.

She climbed the first and paused again for breath. The shallow valley between them seemed empty of life. As the bellowing wind died for a moment she heard the thud of the sea.

As she stood there her earlier despair returned. The motor cycle might not be his. He might have taken the opposite direction. Or — she could no longer suppress the fear — she might already be too late.

Until this moment her one defence had been Robbie — whatever Michael's state of mind she had felt he would not abandon or harm the one creature who had been loyal to him. Now it seemed too frail an assurance to bring comfort. The times he had turned on her had proved the self-destructive qualities of this bitterness. In his agony tonight, the things he loved might well be in more danger than the things he hated.

Forgetting her weariness she ran down into the valley. On her left the cliffs fell sheer to the sea. At some risk, for the wind was fierce again, she peered over the edge but could see nothing but indistinct rocks and the spray of waves.

Lifting her face, wet with a fine drizzle that was now sweeping down she gazed up at the second headland. Time might be all important; should she climb it or return and search the cliffs to the east? The wind seemed to push her forward and she ran up the steep path, digging her heels into the soft turf for a foothold.

Lungs burning for air, she was near exhaustion when she reached the crest. Pin-points of light were stabbing her eyes; as they cleared she saw there was a large clump of bushes fifty yards ahead and to the rear of the path. A fence ran behind them and disappeared into the darkness. That was all: in the range of her vision there was no sign of life.

Tears were now running down her cheeks. About to turn back, she found her attention caught by a movement among the bushes. At first she believed it caused by the wind but as a dark shape separated and moved away from them she saw it was a man who had been sheltering on the lee side. The small black shape that ran after him settled the man's identity beyond doubt.

At first relief drove all else from her

mind. He was safe: the rest took second importance to that. She tried to call him but he was moving away from her and the wind tore away her words.

She started after him. With the path here only a few feet from the cliff edge she took to the soft turf behind it. Michael was drawing nearer the path and suddenly she found something apprehensive in the way the dog was circling him.

She began to run again. He had reached the path and paused there, a thin silhouette against the red-streaked sky. The dog was barking anxiously but he took no notice of it. Terrified again and stumbling with exhaustion she ran towards him. "Michael! Michael; be careful! Come away from the edge."

He stiffened as if a knife had been driven into his back. Then he turned and she saw his face for the first time.

The scar had never known triumph like this. It straddled his face like a great spider, clawing at his cheeks and twisting his lips into a parody of a grill. Only his eyes appeared untouched by it and they stared at her from the grotesque mask with an agony that shocked her.

More frightened than she had ever been she caught his arm and tried to draw him back from the path. "What are you doing here? I've been so worried about you. Come back to the cottage with me — please."

Her touch seemed to break the spell. He jerked his arm away so viciously that she stumbled and almost fell. "Don't touch me! Don't come near me."

"Michael, I know what you're thinking but you're wrong. I didn't give them your address — they got it from a private detective they'd hired to follow me."

"Don't lie. They told me you'd given it to them."

Had they — to make him think she was tired of the affair? Or had his tortured mind imagined it?

"I didn't, Michael. I swear I didn't."

The scar was like an evil spirit possessing him, wanting above all else to hurt her. "You and your bloody pity! Making your sacrifices and pretending you enjoyed coming to see me. I told you in the beginning how much I hated it."

Here was the real wound. Bloody and gaping.

"I haven't made any sacrifices, Michael. Everything I did I wanted to do."

"You expect me to believe that — after what the old woman said? You think I'm a fool as well as a freak?"

"They saw you when you were upset and so got the wrong impression of you. That's why they said what they did. You've admitted yourself what a difference it makes."

"Stop lying!" As he half-stumbled in the wind she thought he was going to strike her. "You told them I was half-crazy and as ugly as Satan, and they came to confirm it. The old woman said so."

With the crimson wound of sky behind him and the dark sea below, she had a feeling of disembodiment, as if she were a spirit fighting to save another from evil. "How could I say such things to them when I've grown to care for you so much? If your bitterness didn't blind you, you'd see I was telling the truth."

His eyes betrayed his desire to believe her before the scar, fighting for dominance, twisted his face beyond recognition. "A year ago I'd got it all beaten. There wasn't any contact — it was over. Then you

had to come along with your platitudes.
Never mind how much it hurts, you said
. . . you have to feel to live. Learn to
trust people — learn to trust me . . . "
His voice rose over the howl of the
wind. "Jesus Christ, after the game you've
played on me I couldn't trust God and all
His angels."

20

AS he took a threatening step towards her she accepted for the first time her life might be in danger.

"You're wrong about me. As soon as I found out what they'd done I drove straight out to see you. Why would I do that if I didn't care about you or if I'd given you away?"

"Why? Because you got scared when you heard what happened. You thought you could kick the animal out when you'd finished playing with it but then you got a stab of conscience. I always said you were a gutless hypocrite."

The thud of a wave below made the cliff tremble. "Let's go back to the cottage, Michael," she begged. "If we must quarrel, let's quarrel there."

"We're not going anywhere. It was right what I said last week — you're worse than any of the others out there. You pretend — they don't even bother. Give me a down-and-out bastard to a flabby saint any time."

"You're afraid to believe me, aren't you, for fear of getting hurt again. You don't need to be. John's mother couldn't have been more wrong about my feelings for you."

"Your feelings for me? Pity! Curiosity! A sick animal to play with when you were bored! I hate you, you bitch. You and all your hypocritical kind."

She made a massive effort to conquer her fear. "Do you hate me or are you just terribly hurt?" When he did not answer she moved forward and laid a hand on his arm. "I swear to you I didn't tell them, Michael. I was as shocked as you when I found out what they'd done. Please come with me now. It's getting late and we've a long walk back to the car."

As he jerked away again the battle within him seemed to reach its climax. He turned towards the sea and she heard him cry something that was lost in the howl of the wind. He took a step forward, whether voluntarily or because of the wind she never knew. Then, as the dog gave an anxious bark, he turned suddenly and began walking back along the path.

He hardly spoke a dozen words to her in the fifteen minutes it took them to reach the car. Nor did he pay any attention to the relieved Robbie who kept leaping up against him. The agony within him seemed to have burned out and left behind an apathy that was in its way as frightening. By the time they reached the car the wound of sky had closed and the cliffs were in darkness. Afraid to allow him out of her sight she begged him to leave the motor cycle behind.

"I'll drive you out first thing in the morning to fetch it. It should be safe enough if you put it in that clump of bushes over there."

Expecting an objection, she took fresh alarm from his indifference. "What's it matter? Leave it where it is."

His mood was unchanged when they reached the cottage. Discovering he had not eaten that evening she prepared sandwiches and a cup of cocoa for him. He sipped at the cocoa but showed no interest in the food. He looked and acted as if he were suffering some mental trauma and her fear grew that her victory on the cliffs had been won only at heavy cost.

There was one question she badly needed to ask. She lit a cigarette and put it into his hand. "Tell me something, Michael. What made you go to the cliffs tonight?"

His eyes were staring at the threadbare carpet in front of his chair. "I don't remember. For a walk, I suppose."

"Had you been there long before I came?"

"I don't know."

"But you did intend to come back here tonight, didn't you?"

His dead eyes lifted. "What?"

"I said you did intend to come back here after your walk?"

He frowned, then nodded. "Yes, I suppose so."

His bitterness was preferable to this, she thought. She knelt down beside his chair and took one of his hands in her own. "There's something else I want you to tell me. What exactly did my husband and his mother say to you? Can you remember?"

The jerk of protest she expected did not come. "He didn't say very much."

"You mean it was his mother who did most of the talking?"

"Yes."

"She didn't understand, Michael. She's a woman with no imagination."

To her surprise his head shook slowly. "No. She understood more than he did."

"Understood what?"

His low voice barely reached her. "She saw the self-pity in me as well as my damned twisted face. After that she was certain we hadn't had an affair."

"That was the reason you attacked me on the cliffs, wasn't it?" she said quietly.

His attempt to laugh made her wince. "It's typical, isn't it? I blame you — I blame everybody — for being a snivelling failure on top of everything else. That's what they made me realize today — that all this time I've been hating the wrong things and the wrong people. The thing I should have hated and despised is myself."

She took a deep breath and tried to make him face her. "How can you blame yourself for what happened to you in the past? Can't you see how unreasonable it is?" When he did not answer her, her voice sharpened. "Michael! Are you listening to me?"

He was not: he appeared to have suddenly withdrawn into a cold, bleak world of his own. As she tried to arouse him, the burning cigarette in his fingers fell to his knees and then to the floor. She waited for him to pick it up but he made no move. As she bent down for it his expression sent a chill through her.

"Michael, don't frighten me like this. Talk to me. I want to help you."

Again he did not move or answer. She thought of his happiness a week earlier and bitterness almost choked her. What did they expect her to do with him now? Leave him to the mercy of his despair?

She walked across the room and switched off the light. In the darkness she heard the yawn and scuffle of the dog as it settled down again in its basket. When the red glow of the oil heater had spread across the room she went over to the settee.

"Michael. Come over here."

His head lifted slowly. "What do you want?"

"I want you to come here and sit with me."

It was a full fifteen seconds before he obeyed. Reaching out, she pressed him back against the cushions. "Lie down. Alongside me."

He lay motionless, his white face staring up at her. She bent over him and laid a hand on his scarred cheek. "You didn't believe what I told you on the cliffs, did you? About how much you meant to me?"

His head shook. "You said it to get me home. So why pretend otherwise?"

In the glow of the heater her eyes were fathomless. "Perhaps I did — but I still meant it. You have to start believing there are some people you can trust, Michael."

Before he could answer she bent lower and pressed her mouth to his. As he gave a violent start she took one of his arms and put it around her. Then, cupping a hand to his face, she ran her lips over the scar and the tensed nerves around it.

In the red glow of the lamp the dog's velvet eyes were watching them. Outside the wind had turned fitful, quiet at one moment, gusting against the window the next. His once bitter face was now as vulnerable as that of a young boy as he stared up at her. As her fingers moved down to his cheeks she felt a wetness there.

His arm seemed afraid to tighten around her and when his eyes closed she believed he had fallen asleep. Afraid to disturb him she waited as long as possible before her aching arms forced her to adjust her position. Sitting up for a moment she removed her sweater. As she turned back she saw his eyes had opened. Smiling, she bent over him again. "Did you sleep?"

He shook his head. She kissed him and when he did not respond she ran his arms down her body, held them to her breasts, and then pressed herself against him. She could feel his desire now and yet his response remained tentative, as if the scar, aware of its new danger, were holding him back.

Her own hands moved down his body. As she touched him he cried out and his lips acknowledged her, yet when she discarded her clothes he still seemed hesitant to possess her.

Gently she slid beneath him, whispering,

wooing, her hands running through his hair and down his naked back. Kissing him, she then reached beneath him to his shuddering flanks. Whispering, smiling, she drew him towards her while his pale, stunned face stared down. He hesitated a last time when he reached her, then, as her arms urged him forward, their bodies were suddenly one.

Afterwards he lay alongside her. Her emotions were strong and complex but there was no sense of guilt among them. In the glow of the heater Robbie stirred, licked himself, and setled down again with a sigh.

She believed Michael had fallen asleep when he lifted his head and moved away. Her body felt cold where he had been and she pressed closer to him again. He turned back to her, and with his head resting on the same cushion as herself she could feel his breathing on her cheek. She was glad he had not spoken. Words seemed of enormous import at that moment and it was wiser to keep silent.

She would have liked to see his face but he was too close to her. Once he muttered something but did not repeat it. Storm-tossed and exhausted by emotion, he was like a man thrown on to some merciful beach. As she listened, his breathing steadied and quietened. She waited another five minutes and drew gently away. As the red glow of the heater touched his face, gratitude flooded through her. In his sleep his features were as peaceful and rested as a child's.

Dressing quietly, she tip-toed upstairs for a blanket which she laid over the sleeping man. She then took the front-door key from his clothes. Tearing a page from her diary, she scribbled him a short note which she left in the centre of the table. By this time Robbie was wagging his tail and scuffling about in his basket. Afraid he would awaken Michael she went over to the dog and under her whispered admonishments he settled down again. Her last act was to turn off the oil heater. Then, latching the front door behind her, she climbed into her car.

21

THE side light of the house had been left on and she had barely entered the drive before John appeared in the porch. Leaving her car outside she walked towards him. He was still fully dressed and his anxious face showed relief on seeing her.

"Is your mother still here?" she asked quietly.

"No. I persuaded her to go home half-an-hour ago, on condition I phoned her as soon as you got back." Closing the door he followed her into the hall. "Have you seen Lindsay?"

"Yes. I've been with him all the evening."

"How is he?"

She turned to him. "Better now, I think, than he was on the cliff top."

He gave a violent start. "The cliff top?"

"Yes. That's where I found him. A few feet from the edge with half a gale blowing."

All the colour had drained from his face. "You can't be serious."

"I'm very serious.

"Are you telling me he tried to commit suicide?"

"I don't know what he was going to do. I don't think he knew himself. Between you and your mother, you did a fine job on him."

He winced. As he took a step towards her she saw his fresh-complexioned face was drawn and contrite. "I'm desperately sorry, darling. I've behaved very badly and I know it."

She gazed at him in dislike. "Sorry for what?"

"For everything. For not believing you and for going to see him. I ought to have trusted you and I'm as ashamed as hell I didn't."

It had to be a handsome apology, she thought. She couldn't be helped by his continued distrust. Her bitterness was like sudden nausea.

"God, they must have fun up there, mustn't they? Pulling and manipulating the strings and watching us jerk and struggle. I suppose it's our pain that gives them their greatest kicks."

He moved anxiously towards her. "What is it? Aren't you feeling well?"

Until that moment she had intended telling him what she had done. Now there seemed no point: enough pain had been inflicted for one day.

"It's nothing," she said, steadying herself. "Just reaction, I suppose." She moved towards the door, then turned. "Is there anything more you want to say before I go?"

"Go?"

"Yes. I'm leaving you, John. You aren't giving me any choice."

His face was very pale. "But I've apologized. I'll go to Michael and apologize to him if you like."

"It wouldn't do any good. I've made up my mind."

"Why? Because you can't forgive me?"

She shook her head slowly. "I don't think forgiveness comes into it. But if that's what you want, I can give it to you."

He looked suddenly defeated. "I see. So it is him after all. Why didn't you admit it before? Wouldn't it have been kinder?"

"It isn't him either, John. Not in the way you mean."

"Then in God's name what is it? Or do you want me to go crazy guessing?"

She gave a small, helpless shrug of her shoulders. "If you don't know now, you never will. I'm not going away from you, John, as much as going away from a way of life."

"A way of life?"

"Yes. From the notion that a man is good and generous if he spends all his time and all his money on people and things that are really only an extension of himself. From the belief that every other human impulse must always take second place to them. I'm running away from marriage, John, not from you."

"I've never heard you complain about the things you've got out of marriage," he said bitterly. "You've never handed me back your clothes or your presents."

She knew it was pain that made him strike out at her. "That's true — I never have. But doesn't that only prove I'm as easily spoiled as anyone else. We can get too much, John, just as we can get too little."

"You talk as if marriage was all taking. What about the sacrifices we have to make?"

The look she gave him brought a flush to his cheeks. "I think I know something about the sacrifices, John. And the biggest is the sacrifice that can't be demanded any longer — not if marriage is to survive the right to self-expression. Like me, more and more people want to find their identities their own way, not have them tailor-made and pushed at one whether they fit or not."

"I never thought I'd made life such hell for you," he said, turning away.

She felt the sudden need to comfort him. "We've had good times together, John. You've given me everything you thought I wanted."

"Except your freedom?"

"Yes," she said quietly. "Except that."

He turned back to her. "But do other men give that to their wives. Do women give it to men, for that matter?"

"I never said they did. That's the size of the tragedy. The world's full of chained people — most of them chained by their own prejudices."

"But you're judging everyone's desires by your own. Most women like to feel themselves possessed."

"I'm not denying that either. But isn't that more reason than ever for disliking a culture that makes them crave such dependence?"

"You're an impossible idealist," he muttered. "You want to change human nature itself."

"I don't believe in human nature any more — not in the way you mean. I believe our attitudes towards love and sex depend on our conditioning. How can it be *natural* to feel guilty for loving someone? Yet we do, because the system has planted guilt in our minds. I believe love and sex are different things, sometimes complementary but just as often in conflict, and I want to sweep away all the cant and humbug about them and to start again. So that at least our children won't grow up to be ashamed of loving."

His laugh was pure bewilderment. "Who would ever get married if they thought like this? What would happen to children in your world of free love?"

"I never mentioned free love and I never asked for the abolition of marriage. I'm saying its concepts and the sacraments responsible for them ought to be changed. Safeguards can still be left in — we don't need to serve prison writs on one another to take care of our children's interests."

As he winced she hated herself. And yet, she thought wearily, wasn't that what the whole affair was about? Too tight a rein and you kicked out. And sometimes found yourself kicking out even after you had broken free.

His voice interrupted her thoughts. "What use are safeguards for children if there isn't a stable society to enforce them? You seem to forget marriage as we know it is the very cornerstone of our society."

She wondered if it were worth going on, then decided it was the least she owed him. "That's another difference between you and me, John. You're satisfied with our society and I'm not. I hate the way we use our money to buy ourselves more gadgets and then close our door on the world while we play with them. I want a complete change in our values. I want us to stop asking ourselves how many new cars or television sets we've built this year compared to the Americans, and ask ourselves instead how many more outstretched hands we've taken, white, brown, or black. I want us to stop using our strength and intelligence to defeat the other man and to use them instead to haul him back to his feet. I'm like the students we read about — I want a new world too. But unlike them I don't think you can change society from the top — not without violence which would make you as callous as the people you depose. To me it's the millions of units that make up the whole you have to change. If they're selfish, the state's selfish, no matter who governs it."

"You're talking about people now, aren't you? Not marriage."

"I'm talking about both. I believe marriage as it exists is a wonderful excuse for us all to be selfish without shame. Millions of individuals, all with something to contribute to humanity, and yet all locked up in their millions of tiny boxes. Spending more and more on them so that the walls get thicker and thicker. There's no cold in there, there's no wind and rain — so very soon there's no humanity either. And yet they keep on telling us this is the cornerstone of our society. Not only you — every institution in the land claims it. I'm not saying there shouldn't be marriage — perhaps we do all need a refuge and our children a home. But as there's a God I'm sure it should never be an entire way of life and that's what we've made it."

He appeared about to answer, then gave a lost shake of his head. Her eyes were held by a cheap plate on the wall above his left shoulder. Hand-painted, with lakes and mountains, it was a souvenir of their first trip abroad together and one she had never found the heart to throw away. The sight of it brought her a feeling of panic. You lived with a man for years and a part of him became a part of you, and nothing could change that no matter if you went to the far ends of the earth. So what defence had one against the memories? The subtle avengers that would creep upon one over the years and jab with their tiny, thirsting daggers?

Her eyes closed against the pain. The

one thing the world was liberal with, she thought — it was yours to share with anyone. But how different the sanctions on love.

When she opened her eyes again he was standing only a few feet away and there were lines on his face she had never seen before. "Let's start again," he pleaded. "I promise it'll be different this time."

Nothing in her life had been harder to say. "Darling, this is tonight. There's next week, next month, next year, and all the years that might follow. There's your mother and all your friends. Do you think they would let us change? They'd scratch my eyes out first."

"After what's happened tonight, do you think I'm likely to listen to them?"

"You can't keep malice quiet, John. Not even if the walls are ten feet thick. I'm not doing this only for myself. If I lived the life I need to live, it isn't only they who would make trouble between us. You would find it difficult to accept too, and you'd be desperately unhappy."

"Am I going to be any happier if you leave me?

"Yes, you are. You won't believe it now

but in the long run it's better for you."

Pain made him strike at her for the last time. "It wouldn't be so easy if you had children, would it?"

Easy! Dear God, did he think it was that? "No," she said quietly. "It wouldn't be so easy. Perhaps that's why I want a world where partings like this need never happen."

Outside on the porch he made his last appeal. "Don't make a decision tonight — wait a few days until things settle. It doesn't matter if you stay with Michael in the meantime — after what's happened I'll understand. But please give yourself time to think."

It was not easy to believe what she was hearing. "Thank you for saying that, John. It's something I won't forget."

As she moved towards the steps he hesitated, then suddenly caught her by the arm. Although his voice was low it was touched with desperation. "There's one thing you must do for me. Whatever happens — whatever you finally decide to do you will take care of yourself, won't you? I must be sure of that."

Suddenly she could not see him for

tears. The watchfulness, the jealousy, the resentment: these things he had once carried almost as a badge of pride. This giving, this caring, this emotion of almost furtive embarrassment — Dear God, could he not see that at this moment he was a man giving evidence of his love?"

Reaching up, she kissed his pale face. "I promise, darling. And you do the same for me. Always."

His hand held her arm for a last moment as she turned away. "I'm sorry, Sarah. More sorry than you'll ever know."

She could not look back at him. "It's I who should be sorry, darling. Try to forgive me and pity me a little. It's such a lonely thing to see life my way."

She remembered little of that last drive to the cottage. Unable to face her pain or to contemplate the future, she concentrated only on things of the moment: the half-moon that was silvering the roads, the first leaves of autumn that the gusting wind kept sweeping past her headlights.

There was no challenge from the dog as she approached the cottage door and she decided it had recognized the sound of her car. Taking the key from her handbag, she let herself inside. All was in darkness and the continued silence made her pause. As she listened her heart began to thud apprehensively and she ran down the narrow passage.

The living room was in darkness except for a wide beam of moonlight that fell across the settee and the floor. Mouth dry, she paused in the doorway to listen again. For a few seconds the silence hurt her ears. Then she heard a scuffle, followed by a low whine from the puzzled dog.

The sound released her and she ran over to the settee. Michael was lying as she had left him and as she bent down she heard his low, steady breathing. As she straightened in relief the dog came over to her and nuzzled its wet nose against her legs.

She was trembling as she bent down to pat it. "Go back to sleep, you funny old thing," she whispered. "I shan't disturb you again."

She crossed over to the window. Although threatened by clouds, the moon was floating clear in a wide pool of sky. The garden was alive with silver lights and as she watched two bats flittered among them before vanishing into the heath.

Turning, she gazed back at the sleeping man. With so much happening to her since she had left the cottage, it was difficult to believe he had slept all the time like a child.

Drawing the curtains across the window she lit the oil heater. The dog entered his basket, scuffled round in it for a moment, then settled down. She fetched a blanket from upstairs and took the armchair near the settee. As she closed her eyes her distress and fears leapt at her but she drove them back. She had done what she had done: tomorrow was time enough to consider the road ahead. Tonight she was resting in a small oasis and she would detach the moment from time so that neither the past nor the future could harm it. Pulling the blanket up to her shoulders she closed her eyes again while the red glow of the heater spread towards her and outside a dog-fox made its call to the moon.

CLOUD OVER MALVERTON
Nancy Buckingham

Dulcie soon realises that something is seriously wrong at Malverton, and when violence strikes she is horrified to find herself under suspicion of murder.

AFTER THOUGHTS
Max Bygraves

The Cockney entertainer tells stories of his East End childhood, of his RAF days, and his post-war showbusiness successes and friendships with fellow comedians.

MOONLIGHT AND MARCH ROSES
D. Y. Cameron

Lynn's search to trace a missing girl takes her to Spain, where she meets Clive Hendon. While untangling the situation, she untangles her emotions and decides on her own future.

NURSE ALICE IN LOVE
Theresa Charles

Accepting the post of nurse to little Fernie Sherrod, Alice Everton could not guess at the romance, suspense and danger which lay ahead at the Sherrod's isolated estate.

POIROT INVESTIGATES
Agatha Christie

Two things bind these eleven stories together — the brilliance and uncanny skill of the diminutive Belgian detective, and the stupidity of his Watson-like partner, Captain Hastings.

LET LOOSE THE TIGERS
Josephine Cox

Queenie promised to find the long-lost son of the frail, elderly murderess, Hannah Jason. But her enquiries threatened to unlock the cage where crucial secrets had long been held captive.

THE TWILIGHT MAN
Frank Gruber

Jim Rand lives alone in the California desert awaiting death. Into his hermit existence comes a teenage girl who blows both his past and his brief future wide open.

DOG IN THE DARK
Gerald Hammond

Jim Cunningham breeds and trains gun dogs, and his antagonism towards the devotees of show spaniels earns him many enemies. So when one of them is found murdered, the police are on his doorstep within hours.

THE RED KNIGHT
Geoffrey Moxon

When he finds himself a pawn on the chessboard of international espionage with his family in constant danger, Guy Trent becomes embroiled in moves and countermoves which may mean life or death for Western scientists.

TIGER TIGER
Frank Ryan

A young man involved in drugs is found murdered. This is the first event which will draw Detective Inspector Sandy Woodings into a whirlpool of murder and deceit.

CAROLINE MINUSCULE
Andrew Taylor

Caroline Minuscule, a medieval script, is the first clue to the whereabouts of a cache of diamonds. The search becomes a deadly kind of fairy story in which several murders have an other-worldly quality.

LONG CHAIN OF DEATH
Sarah Wolf

During the Second World War four American teenagers from the same town join the Army together. Forty-two years later, the son of one of the soldiers realises that someone is systematically wiping out the families of the four men.

THE LISTERDALE MYSTERY
Agatha Christie

Twelve short stories ranging from the light-hearted to the macabre, diverse mysteries ingeniously and plausibly contrived and convincingly unravelled.

TO BE LOVED
Lynne Collins

Andrew married the woman he had always loved despite the knowledge that Sarah married him for reasons of her own. So much heartache could have been avoided if only he had known how vital it was to be loved.

ACCUSED NURSE
Jane Converse

Paula found herself accused of a crime which could cost her her job, her nurse's reputation, and even the man she loved, unless the truth came to light.

BUTTERFLY MONTANE
Dorothy Cork

Parma had come to New Guinea to marry Alec Rivers, but she found him completely disinterested and that overbearing Pierce Adams getting entirely the wrong idea about her.

HONOURABLE FRIENDS
Janet Daley

Priscilla Burford is happily married when she meets Junior Environment Minister Alistair Thurston. Inevitably, sexual obsession and political necessity collide.

WANDERING MINSTRELS
Mary Delorme

Stella Wade's career as a concert pianist might have been ruined by the rudeness of a famous conductor, so it seemed to her agent and benefactor. Even Sir Nicholas fails to see the possibilities when John Tallis falls deeply in love with Stella.

MORNING IS BREAKING
Lesley Denny

The growing frenzy of war catapults Diane Clements into a clandestine marriage and separation with a German refugee.

LAST BUS TO WOODSTOCK
Colin Dexter

A girl's body is discovered huddled in the courtyard of a Woodstock pub, and Detective Chief Inspector Morse and Sergeant Lewis are hunting a rapist and a murderer.

THE STUBBORN TIDE
Anne Durham

Everyone advised Carol not to grieve so excessively over her cousin's death. She might have followed their advice if the man she loved thought that way about her, but another girl came first in his affections.

FATAL RING OF LIGHT
Helen Eastwood

Katy's brother was supposed to have died in 1897 but a scrawled note in his handwriting showed July 1899. What had happened to him in those two years? Katy was determined to help him.

NIGHT ACTION
Alan Evans

Captain David Brent sails at dead of night to the German occupied Normandy town of St. Jean on a mission which will stretch loyalty and ingenuity to its limits, and beyond.

A MURDER TOO MANY
Elizabeth Ferrars

Many, including the murdered man's widow, believed the wrong man had been convicted. The further murder of a key witness in the earlier case convinced Basnett that the seemingly unrelated deaths were linked.

A GREAT DELIVERANCE
Elizabeth George

Into the web of old houses and secrets of Keldale Valley comes Scotland Yard Inspector Thomas Lynley and his assistant to solve a particularly savage murder.

'E' IS FOR EVIDENCE
Sue Grafton

Kinsey Millhone was bogged down on a warehouse fire claim. It came as something of a shock when she was accused of being on the take. She'd been set up. Now she had a new client — herself.

A FAMILY OUTING IN AFRICA
Charles Hampton and Janie Hampton

A tale of a young family's journey through Central Africa by bus, train, river boat, lorry, wooden bicyle and foot.

SEASONS OF MY LIFE
Hannah Hauxwell and Barry Cockcroft

The story of Hannah Hauxwell's struggle to survive on a desolate farm in the Yorkshire Dales with little money, no electricity and no running water.

TAKING OVER
Shirley Lowe and Angela Ince

A witty insight into what happens when women take over in the boardroom and their husbands take over chores, children and chickenpox.

AFTER MIDNIGHT STORIES,
The Fourth Book Of

A collection of sixteen of the best of today's ghost stories, all different in style and approach but all combining to give the reader that special midnight shiver.

DEATH TRAIN
Robert Byrne

The tale of a freight train out of control and leaking a paralytic nerve gas that turns America's West into a scene of chemical catastrophe in which whole towns are rendered helpless.

THE ADVENTURE OF THE CHRISTMAS PUDDING
Agatha Christie

In the introduction to this short story collection the author wrote "This book of Christmas fare may be described as 'The Chef's Selection'. I am the Chef!"

RETURN TO BALANDRA
Grace Driver

Returning to her Caribbean island home, Suzanne looks forward to being with her parents again, but most of all she longs to see Wim van Branden, a coffee planter she has known all her life.

DEAD SPIT
Janet Edmonds

Government vet Linus Rintoul attempts to solve a mystery which plunges him into the esoteric world of pedigree dogs, murder and terrorism, and Crufts Dog Show proves to be far more exciting than he had bargained for . . .

A BARROW IN THE BROADWAY
Pamela Evans

Adopted by the Gordillo family, Rosie Goodson watched their business grow from a street barrow to a chain of supermarkets. But passion, bitterness and her unhappy marriage aliented her from them.

THE GOLD AND THE DROSS
Eleanor Farnes

Lorna found it hard to make ends meet for herself and her mother and then by chance she met two men — one a famous author and one a rich banker. But could she really expect to be happy with either man?

BALLET GENIUS
Gillian Freeman and Edward Thorpe

Presents twenty pen portraits of great dancers of the twentieth century and gives an insight into their daily lives, their professional careers, the ever present risk of injury and the pressure to stay on top.

TO LIVE IN PEACE
Rosemary Friedman

The final part of the author's Anglo-Jewish trilogy, which began with PROOFS OF AFFECTION and ROSE OF JERICHO, telling the story of Kitty Shelton, widowed after a happy marriage, and her three children.

NORA WAS A NURSE
Peggy Gaddis

Nurse Nora Courtney was hopelessly in love with Doctor Owen Baird and when beautiful Lillian Halstead set her cap for him, Nora realised she must make him see her as a desirable woman as well as an efficient nurse.

PREJUDICED WITNESS
Dilys Gater

Fleur Rowley finds when she leaves London for her 'author's retreat' in the wilds of North Wales that she is drawn, in spite of herself, into an old tragedy.

GENTLE TYRANT
Lucy Gillen

Working as Ross McAdam's secretary, Laura couldn't imagine why his bitchy ex-wife should see her as a rival.

DEAR CAPRICE
Juliet Gray

Clifford Fortune married Caprice but his brother, Luke, knew the marriage was a mistake. He could allow himself to love Caprice blindly but that would be betraying his own brother.